THE PLAYERS:

GRONK: GRONK IS A YOUNG ... HER BACK ON THE WAYS OF MONSTER ... WAS JUST TOO DARN ADORABLE TO BE SCARY). SHE FINDS ... UMAN WORLD FASCINATING AND IS CURIOUS ABOUT EVERYTHING...

DALE WILCO: DALE WORKS OUT OF HER HOUSE IN A RURAL AREA OF BRITISH COLUMBIA... COMPOSING MUSIC FOR COMMERCIALS AND TV SHOWS. SHE'S A CREATIVE PERSON AT HEART AND HER LONER LIFESTYLE IS THROWN INTO A LOOP WHEN A LITTLE GREEN MONSTER SHOWS UP IN HER LIFE.

HARLI: DALE'S 160 POUND NEWFOUNDLAND. LOVABLE AND EASILY MANIPULATED WHEN OFFERED PIZZA. DALE THINKS THAT HARLI IS LARGE ENOUGH TO BE COUNTED AS LIVING WITH AN ACTUAL PERSON AND MAY HAVE TRIED TO WRITE HER OFF AS A DEPENDENT ON HER TAXES.

KITTY: A CUTE, FUZZY FURBALL WHO CAN TURN FROM BALL OF ENERGY INTO A LAZY LUMP IN .0003 SECONDS. TYPICAL CAT... GREATEST AMBITION IN LIFE IS TO BE CAPTIONED AS A LOLCAT ON THE INTERNET.

KITTEH: GRONK'S PLUSH KITTY

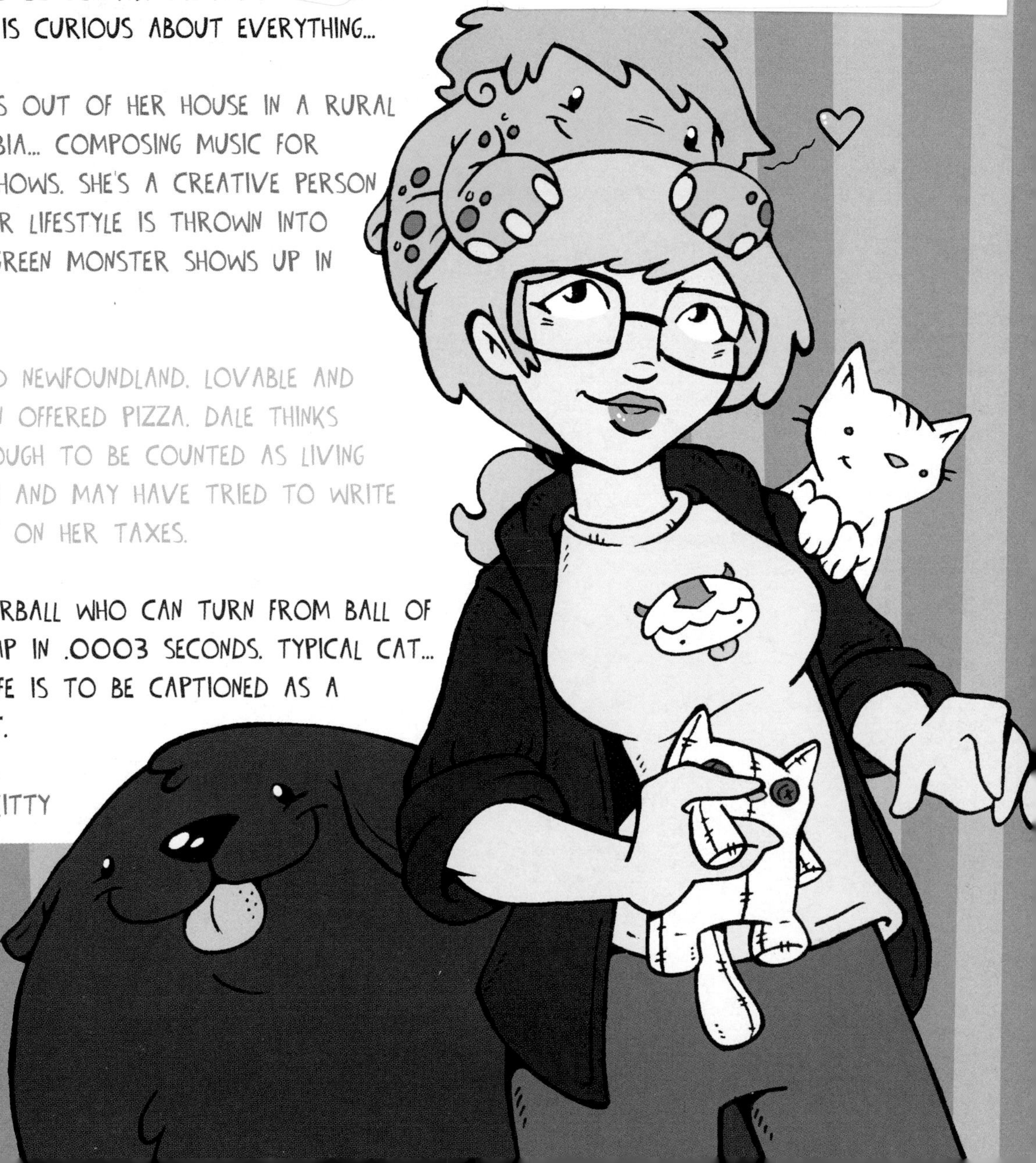

GRONK™
a monster's story
a comic by katie cook

you can find gronk online here: www.gronkcomic.com
you can find katie online here: www.katiecandraw.com
colors for the interior pages provided by the awesome kevin minor

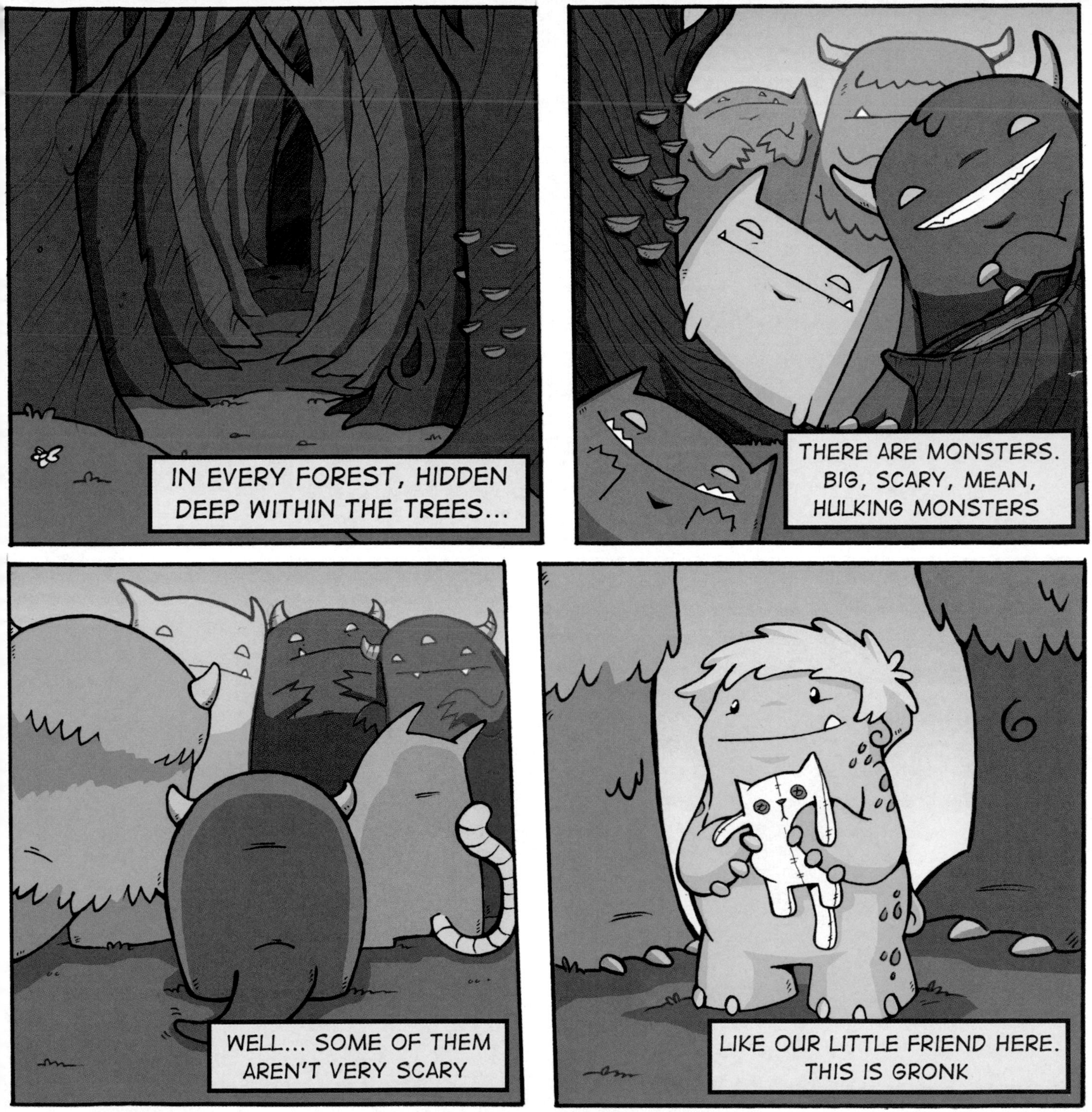
IN EVERY FOREST, HIDDEN DEEP WITHIN THE TREES...
THERE ARE MONSTERS. BIG, SCARY, MEAN, HULKING MONSTERS
WELL... SOME OF THEM AREN'T VERY SCARY
LIKE OUR LITTLE FRIEND HERE. THIS IS GRONK

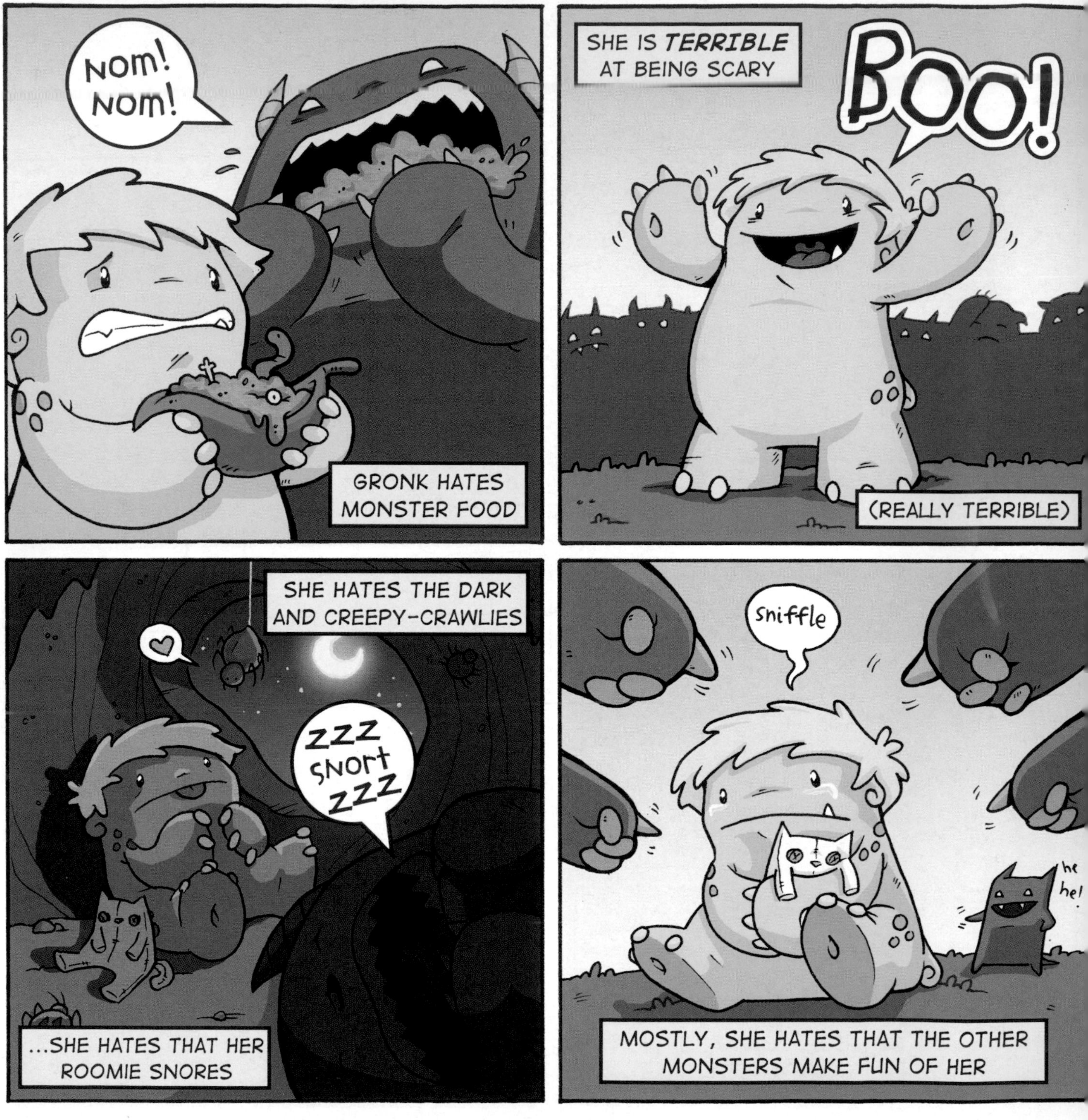
Nom! Nom!
GRONK HATES MONSTER FOOD
SHE IS TERRIBLE AT BEING SCARY
BOO!
(REALLY TERRIBLE)
SHE HATES THE DARK AND CREEPY-CRAWLIES
ZZZ snort ZZZ
...SHE HATES THAT HER ROOMIE SNORES
sniffle
he he!
MOSTLY, SHE HATES THAT THE OTHER MONSTERS MAKE FUN OF HER

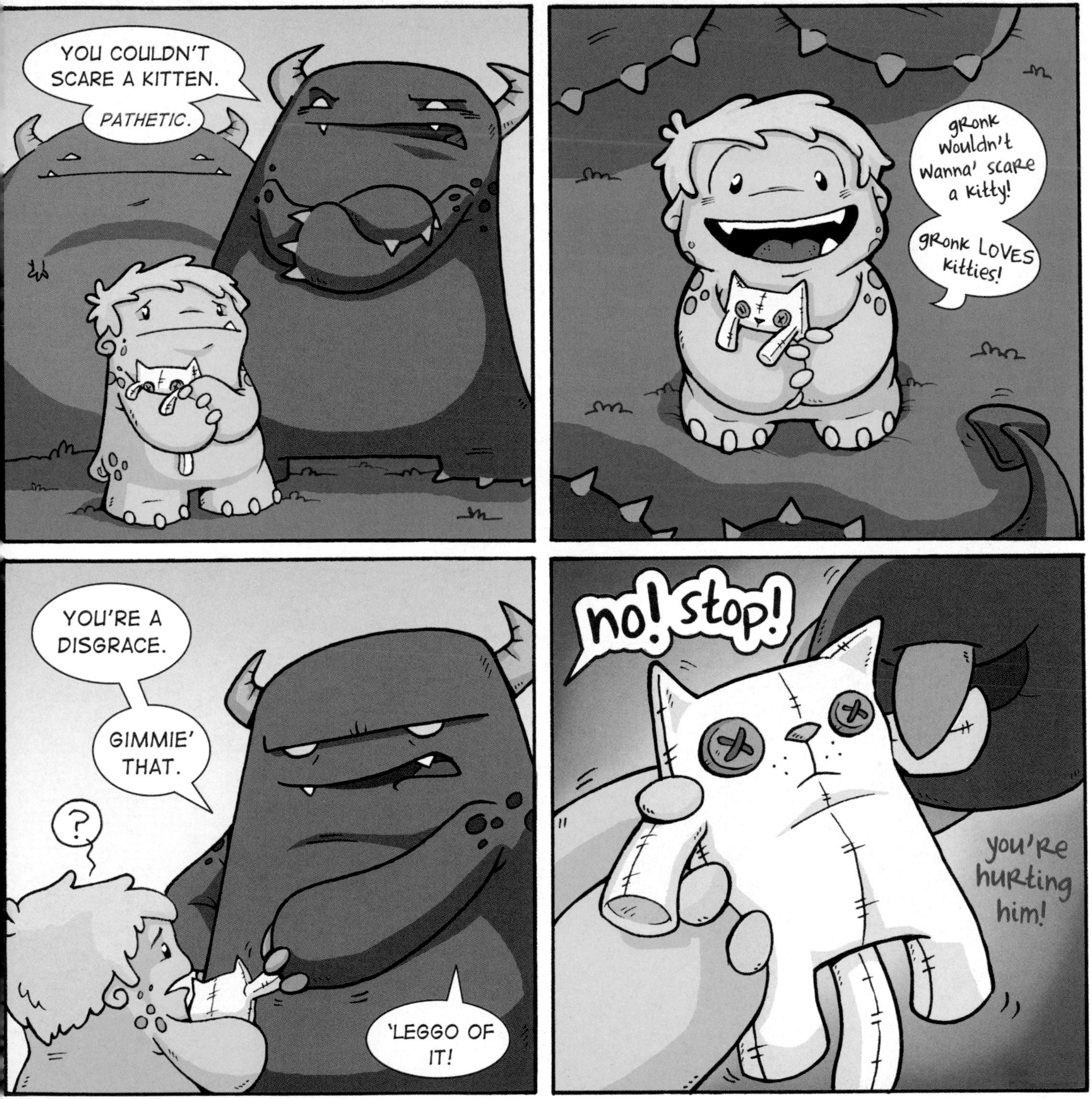
YOU COULDN'T SCARE A KITTEN.
PATHETIC.
gRonk wouldn't wanna' scaRe a kitty!
gRonk LOVES kitties!
YOU'RE A DISGRACE.
GIMMIE' THAT.
?
'LEGGO OF IT!
no! stop!
you're huRting him!

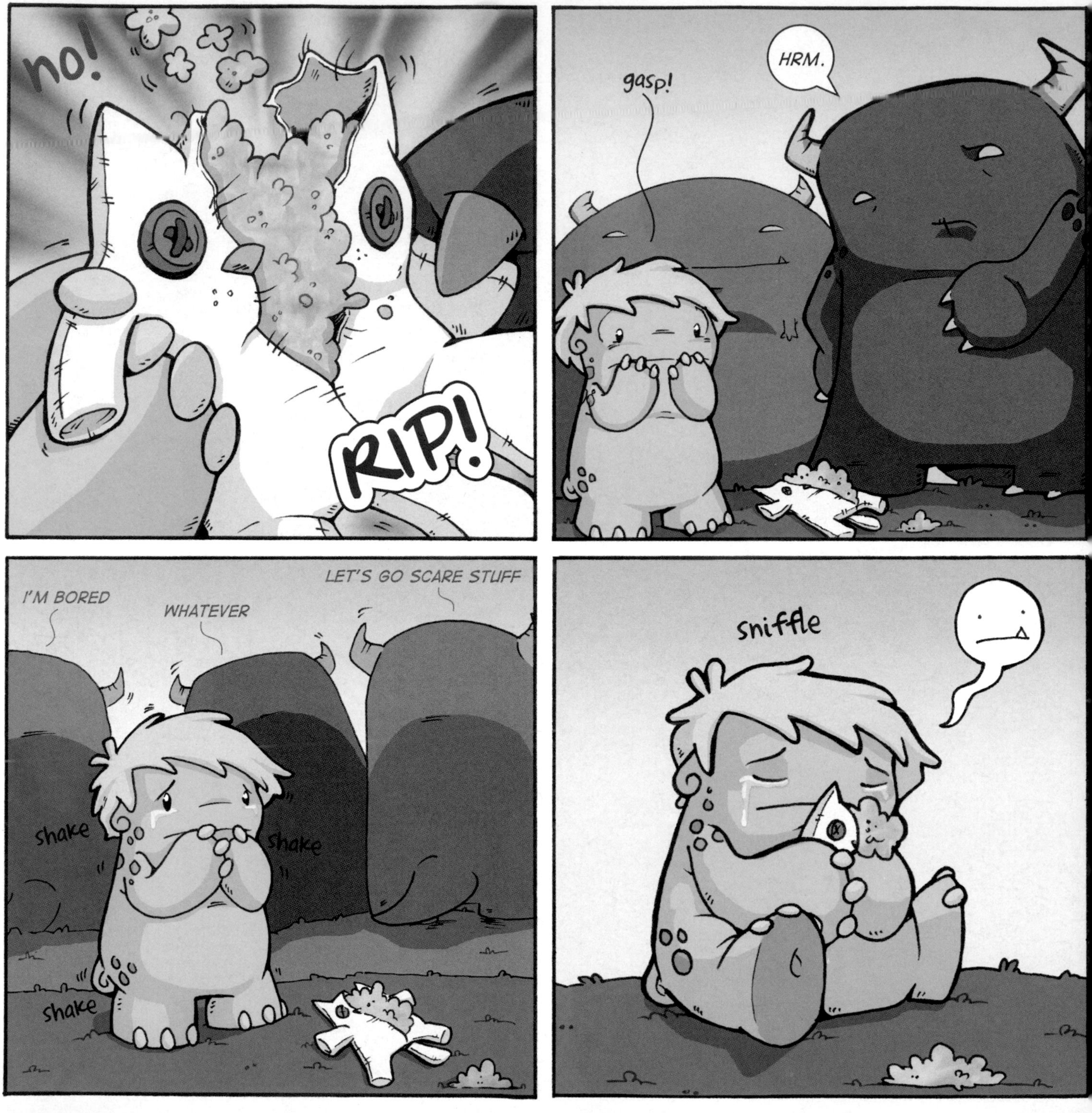
no!
RIP!
gasp!
HRM.
I'M BORED
WHATEVER
LET'S GO SCARE STUFF
shake
shake
shake
sniffle

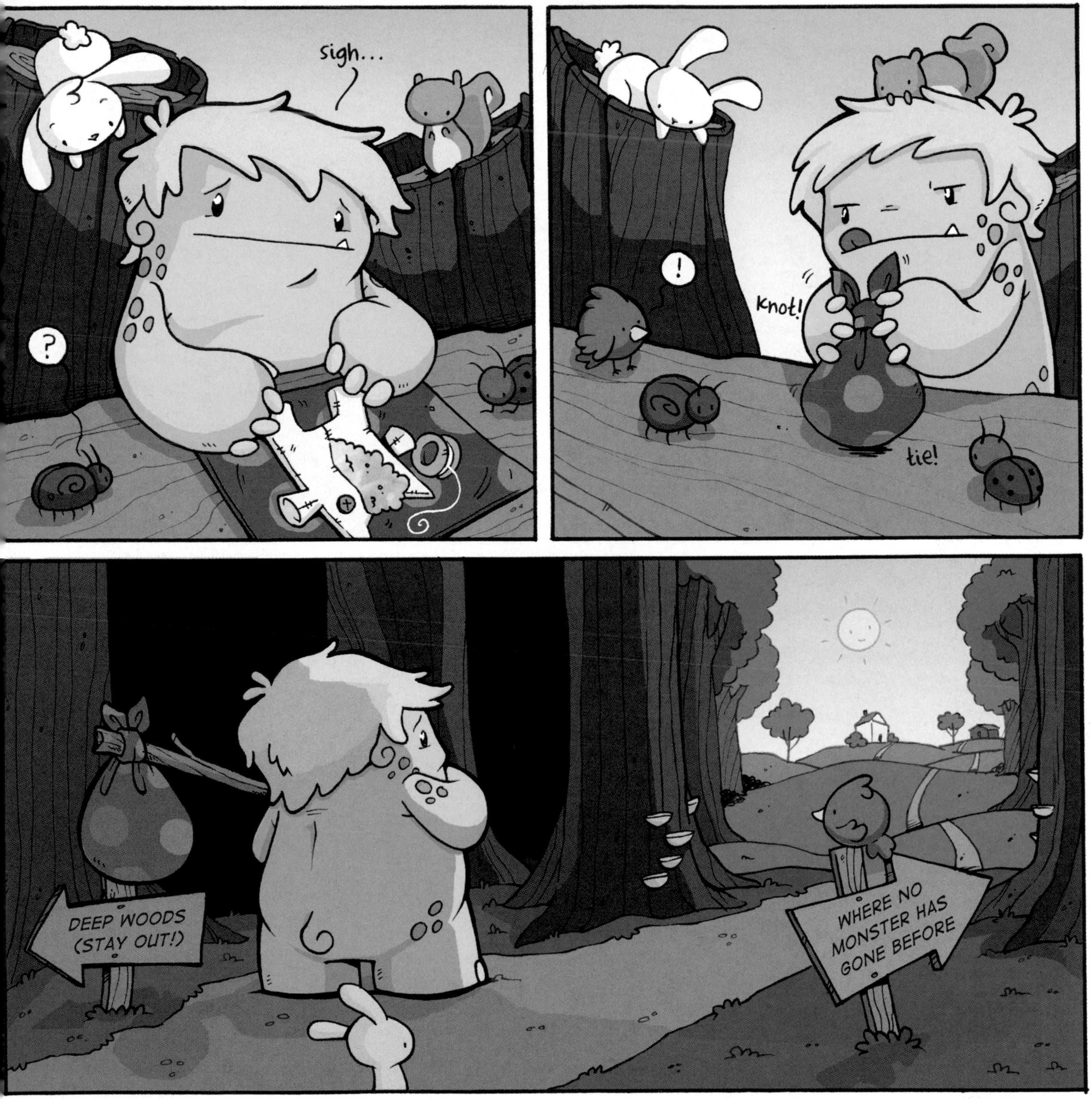
sigh...
?
!
Knot!
tie!
DEEP WOODS
(STAY OUT!)
WHERE NO
MONSTER HAS
GONE BEFORE

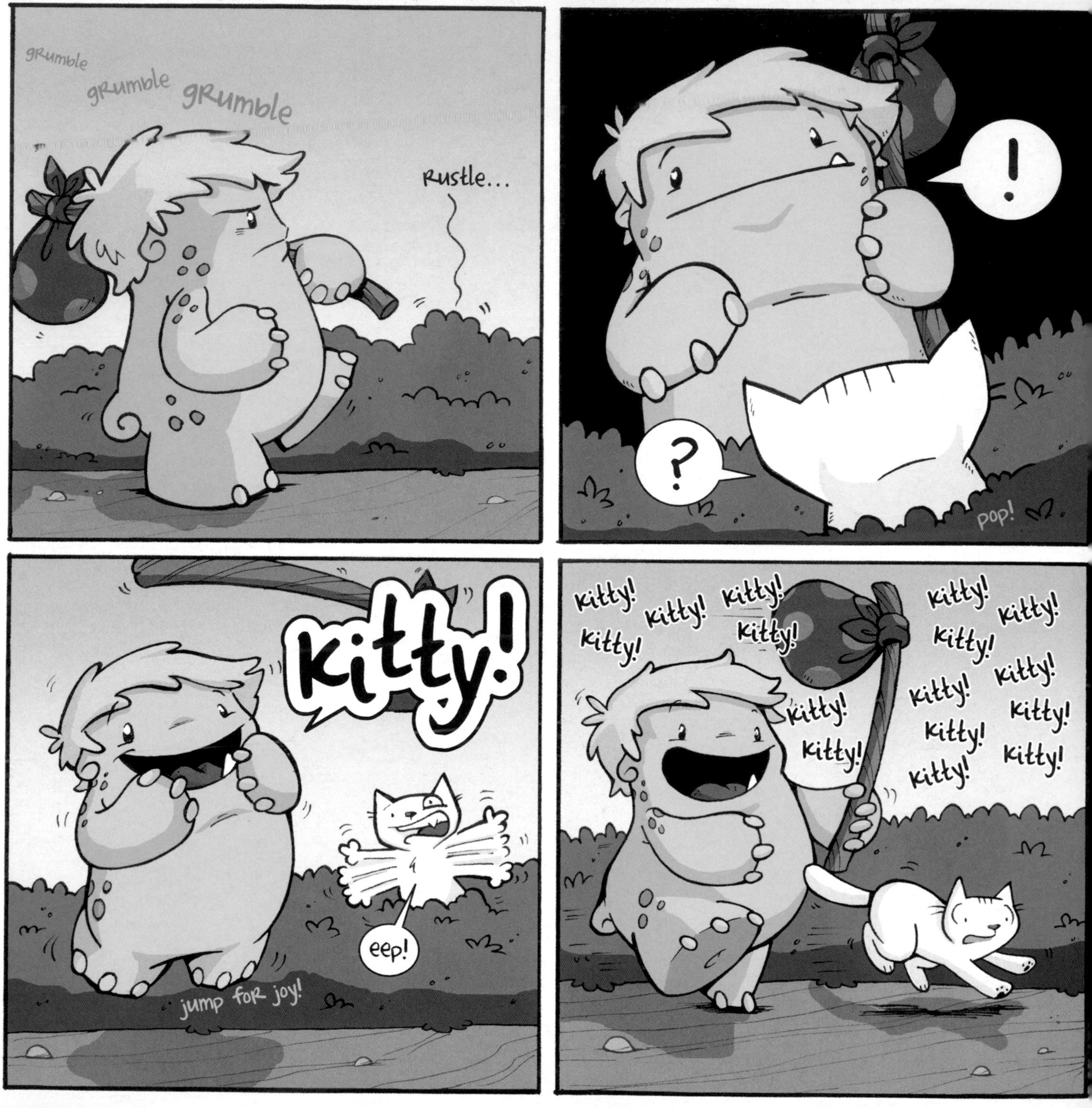
grumble
grumble
grumble
Rustle...
!
?
pop!
kitty!
eep!
jump for joy!
kitty! kitty! kitty! kitty! kitty!
kitty! kitty! kitty! kitty! kitty! kitty! kitty! kitty! kitty! kitty! kitty!

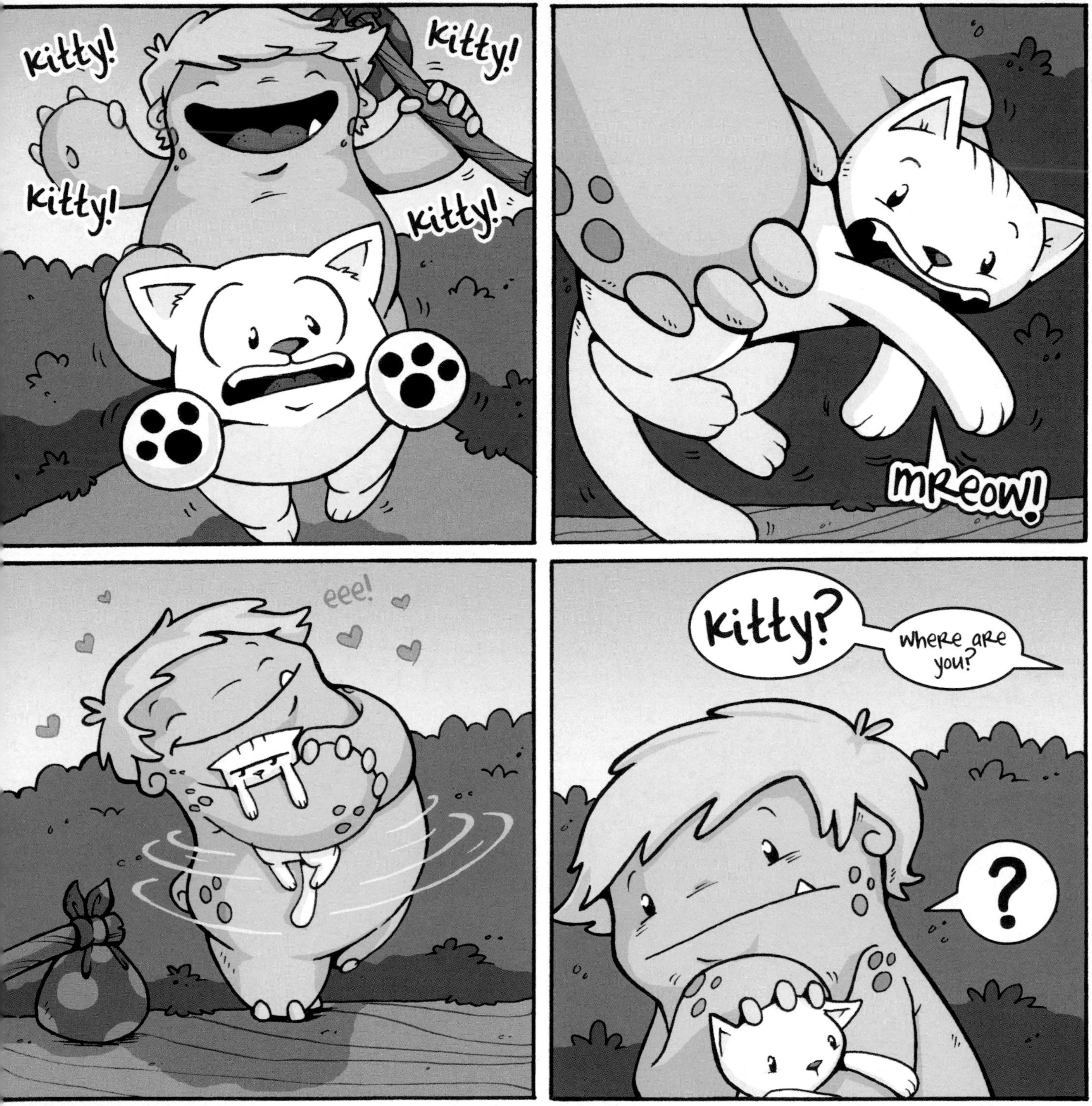
kitty!
kitty!
kitty!
kitty!
mreow!
eee!
kitty?
where are you?
?

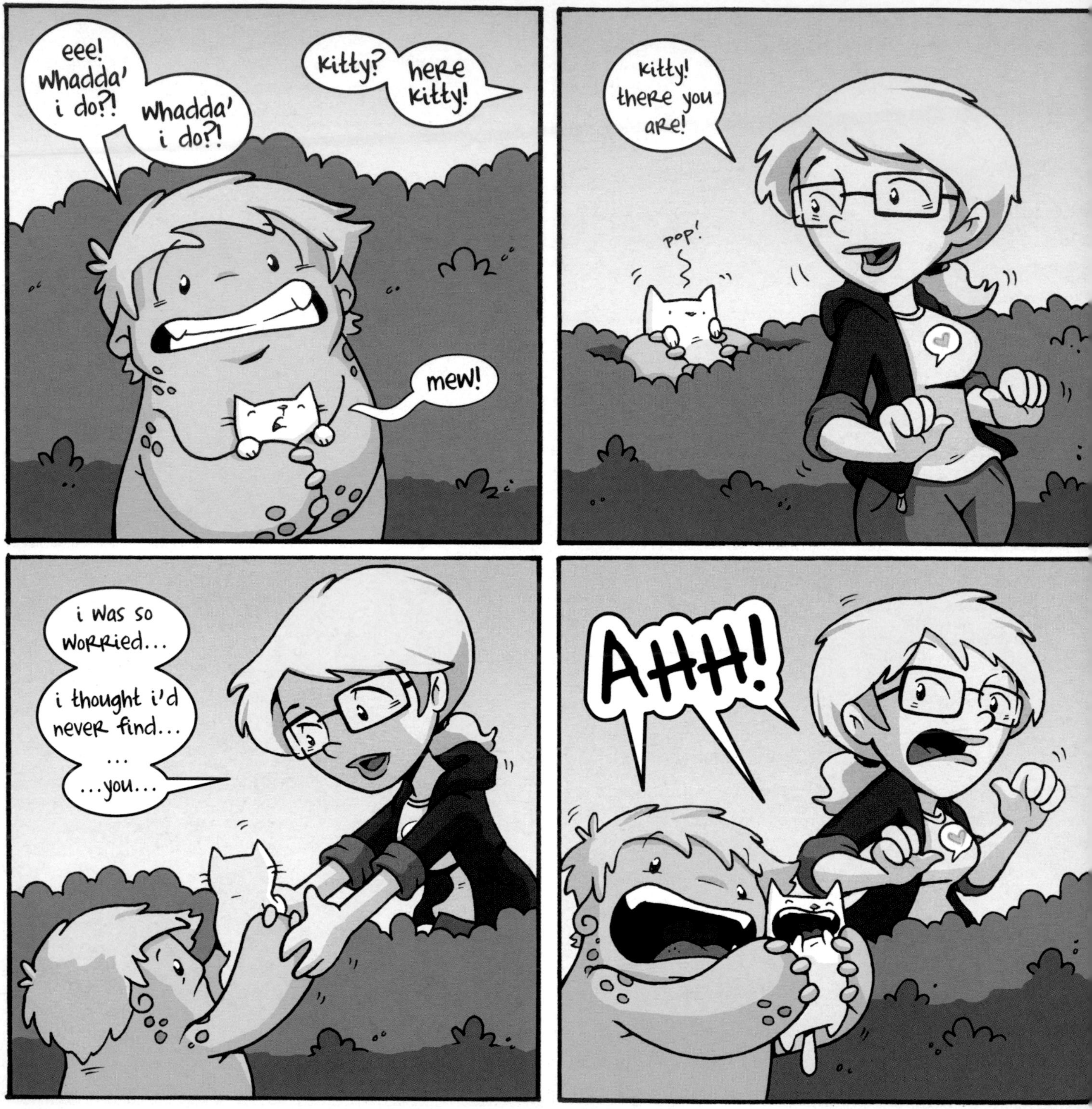
eee! whadda' i do?!
whadda' i do?!
kitty?
here kitty!
mew!
kitty! there you are!
POP!
i was so worried...
i thought i'd never find...
...
...you...
AHH!

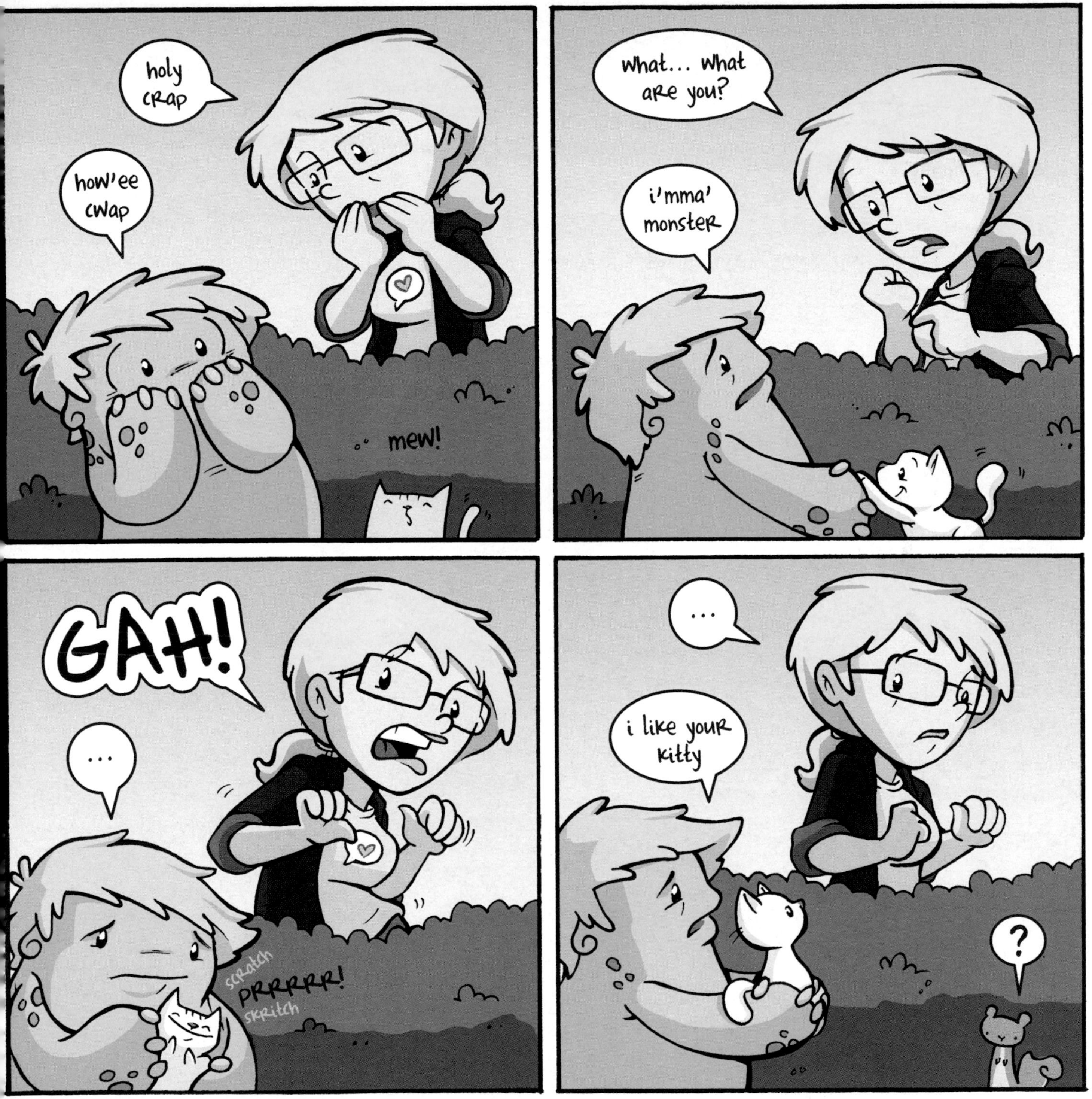
holy crap
how'ee cwap
mew!
what... what are you?
i'mma' monster
GAH!
...
scratch
PRRRRR!
skritch
...
i like your kitty
?

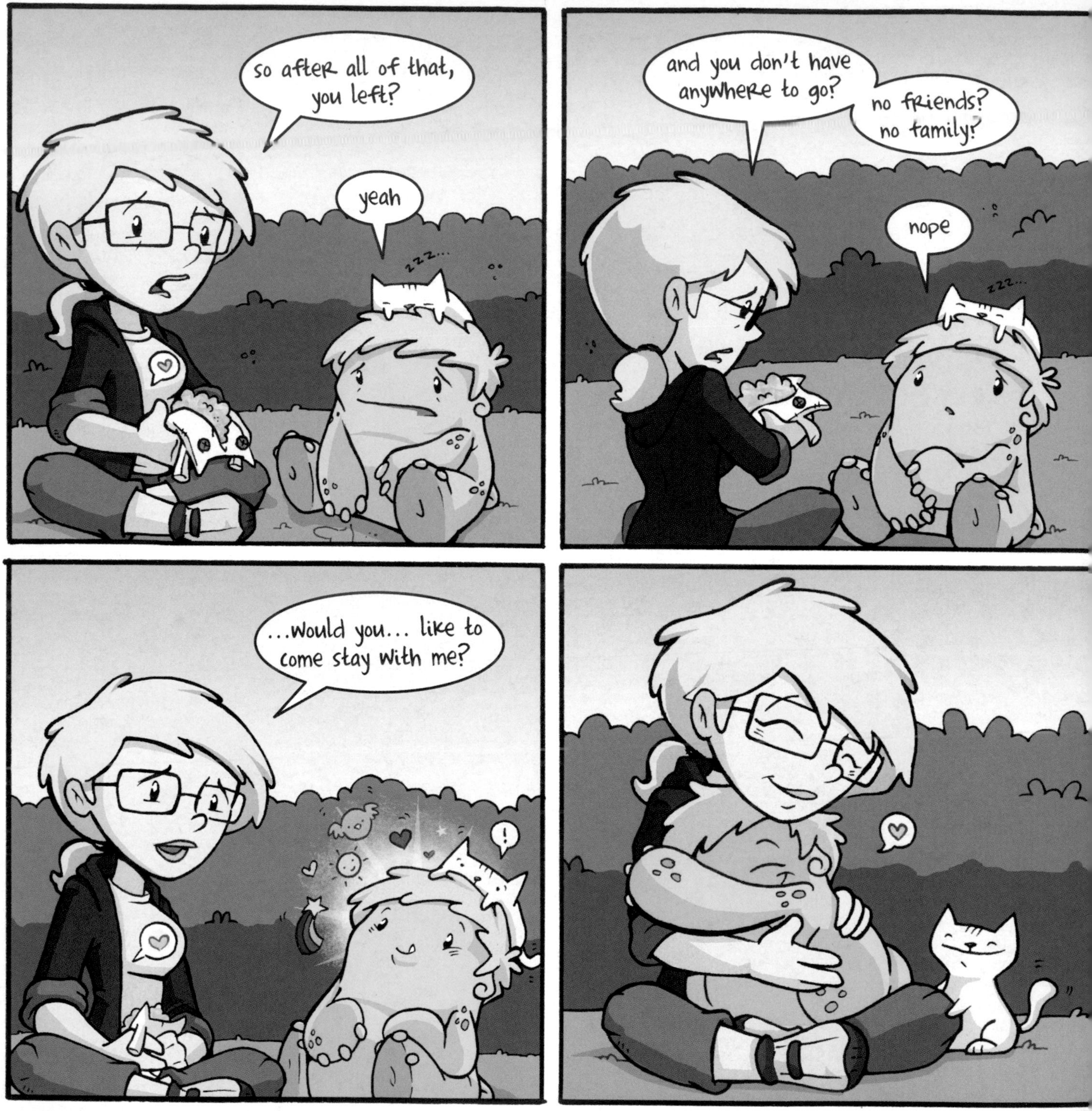
so after all of that, you left?
yeah
zzz...
and you don't have anywhere to go?
no friends? no family?
nope
zzz...
...would you... like to come stay with me?
!

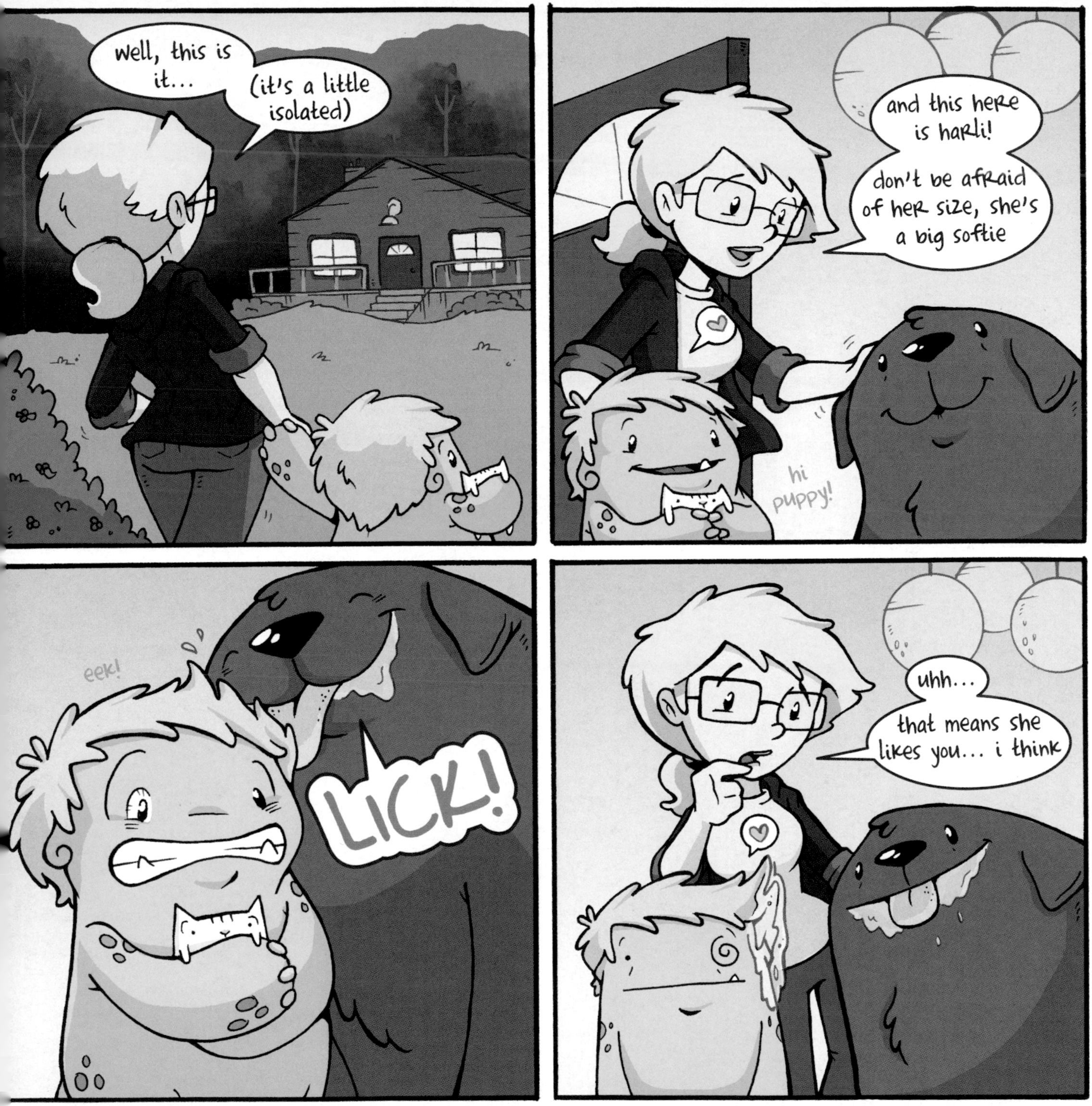
well, this is it...
(it's a little isolated)
and this here is harli!
don't be afraid of her size, she's a big softie
hi puppy!
eek!
LICK!
uhh...
that means she likes you... i think

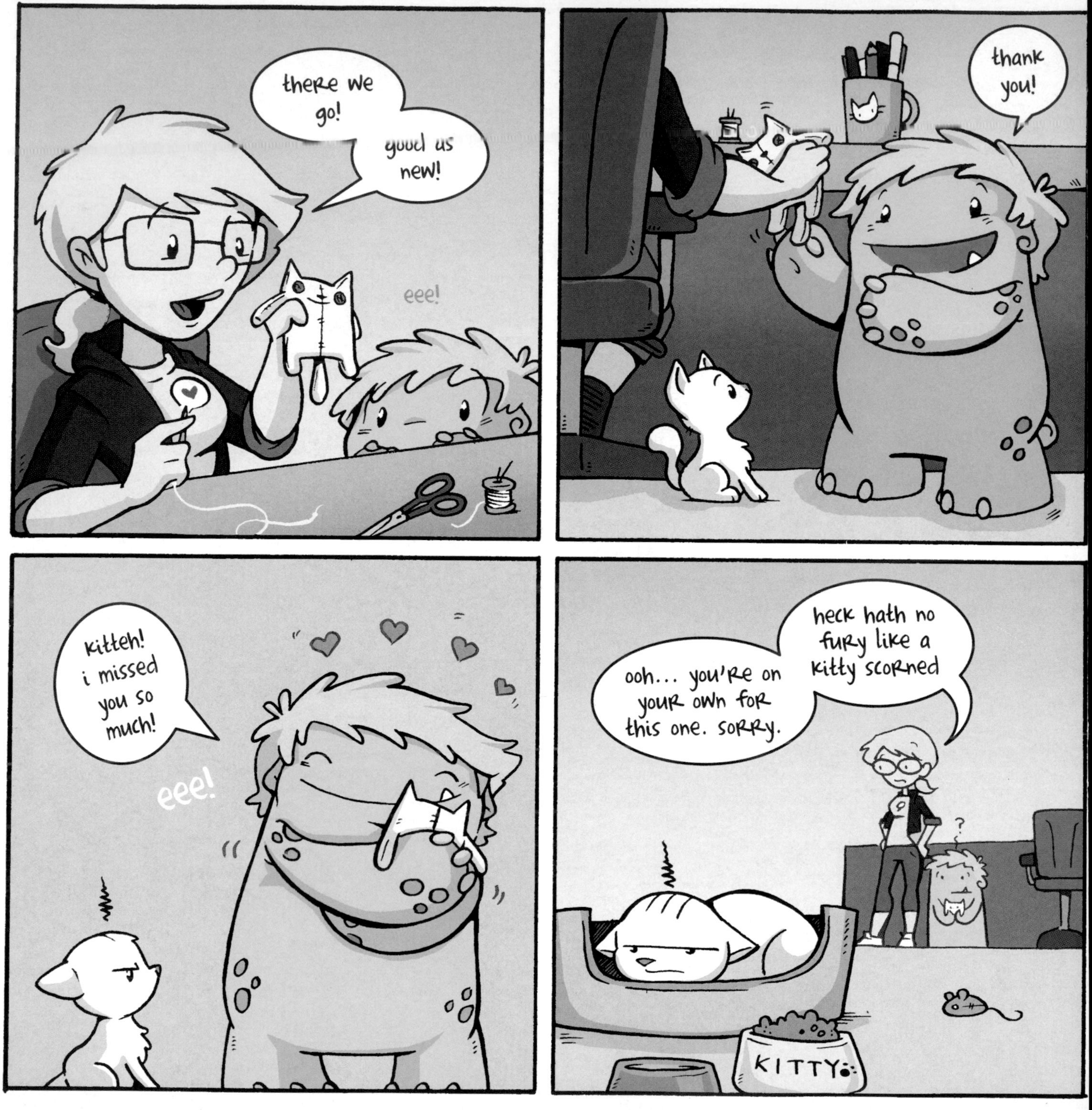
there we go!
good as new!
eee!
thank you!
kitteh! i missed you so much!
eee!
heck hath no fury like a kitty scorned
ooh... you're on your own for this one. sorry.
?
KITTY

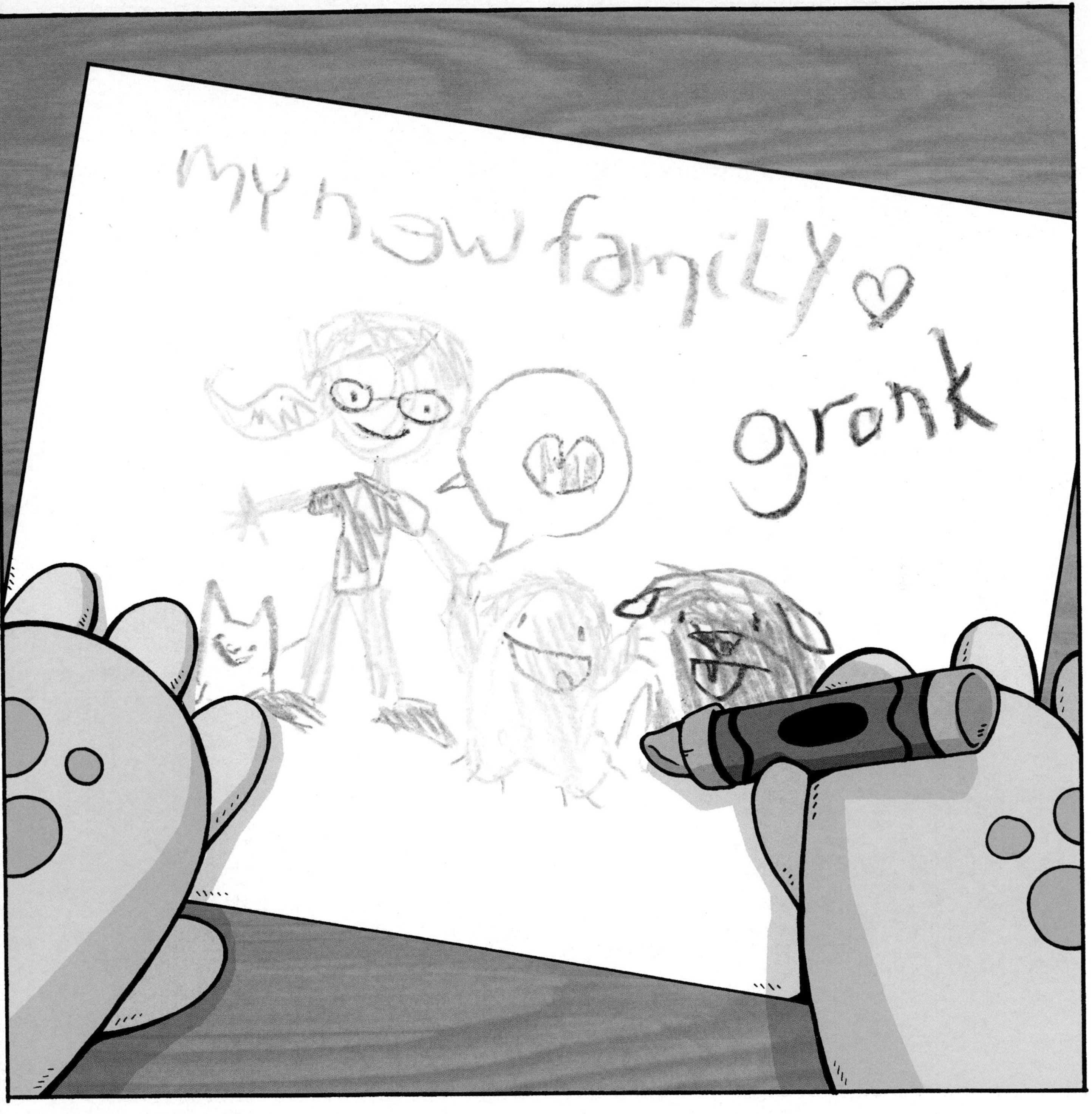
my new family
gronk

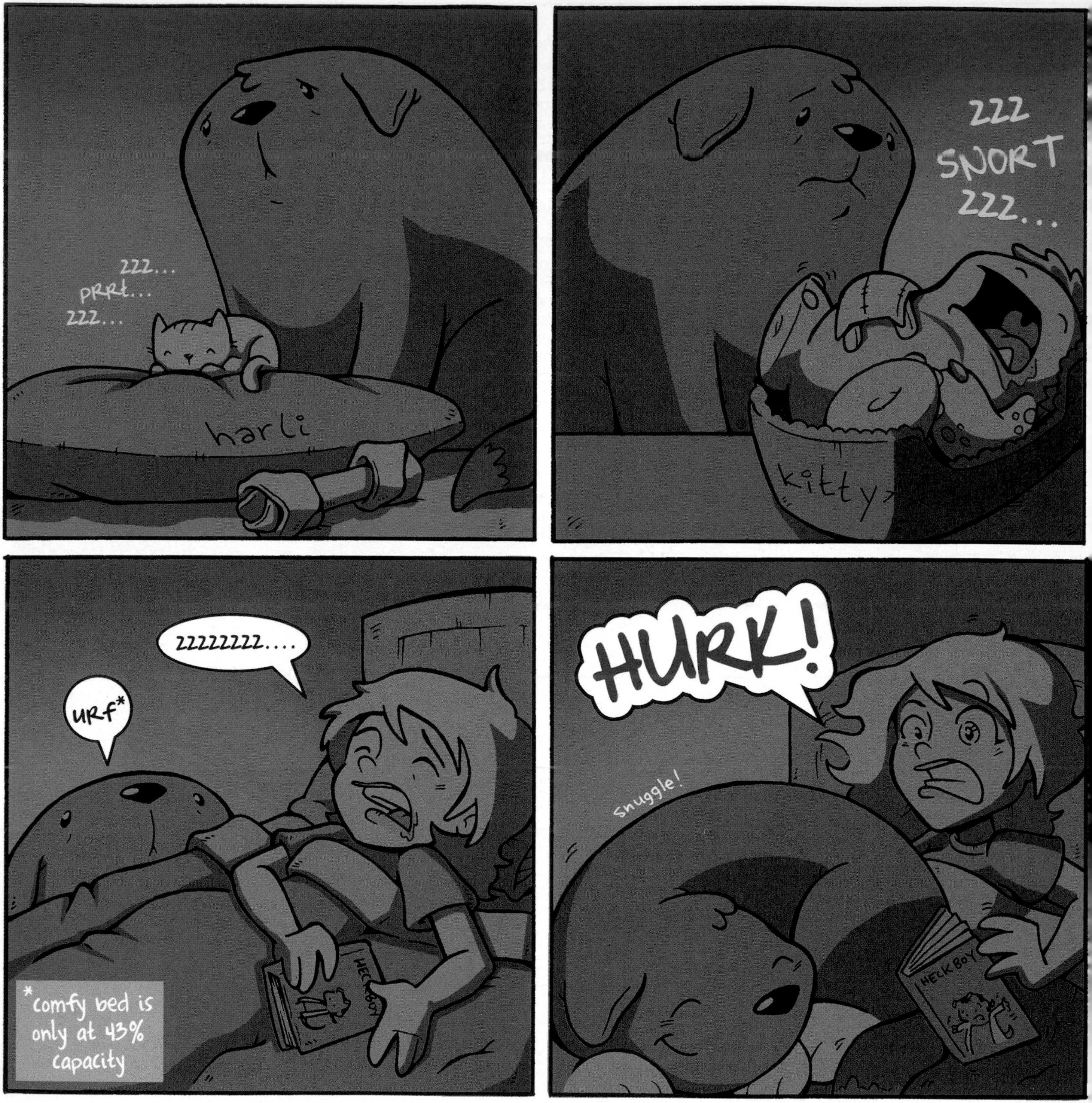
zzz...
prrt...
zzz...
harli
zzz
SNORT
zzz...
kitty
zzzzzzzz....
urf*
HELLBOY
*comfy bed is only at 43% capacity
HURK!
snuggle!
HELLBOY

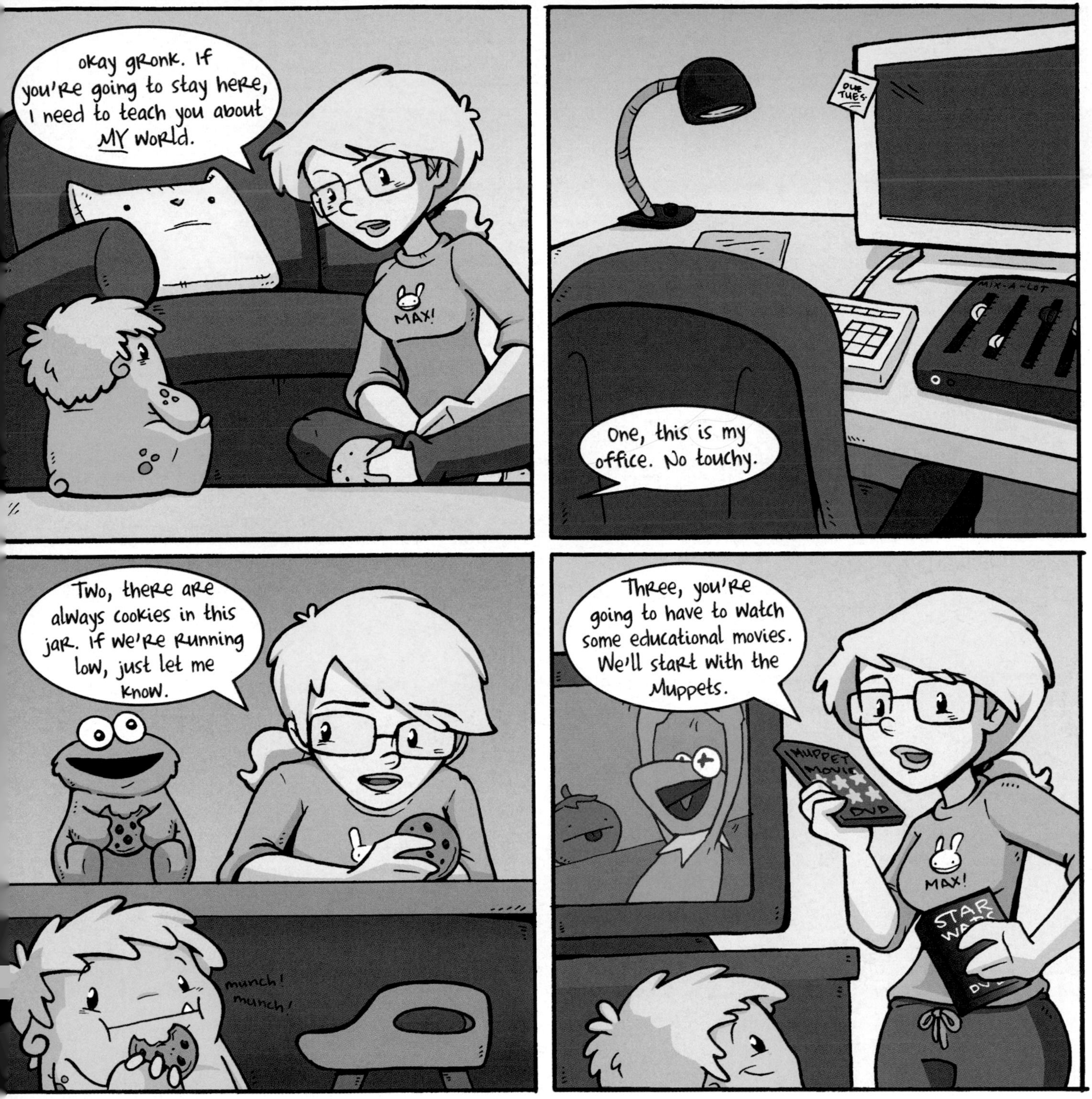
okay gRonk. If you're going to stay heRe, I need to teach you about MY woRld.
One, this is my office. No touchy.
Two, there aRe always cookies in this jaR. If we're Running low, just let me know.
munch! munch!
Three, you're going to have to watch some educational movies. We'll staRt with the Muppets.
MAX!
MUPPET MOVIE DVD

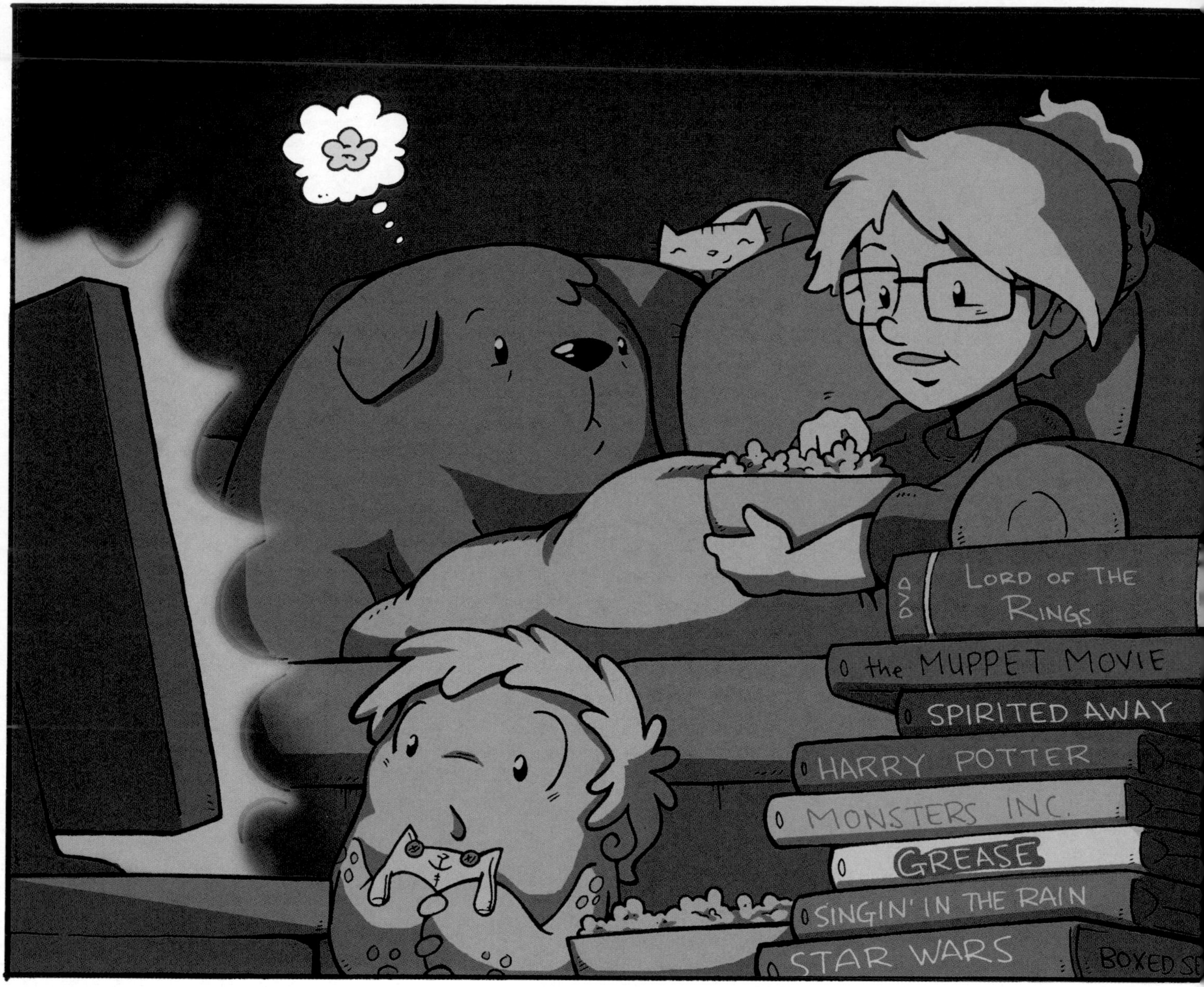
DVD
LORD OF THE RINGS
the MUPPET MOVIE
SPIRITED AWAY
HARRY POTTER
MONSTERS INC.
GREASE
SINGIN' IN THE RAIN
STAR WARS
BOXED

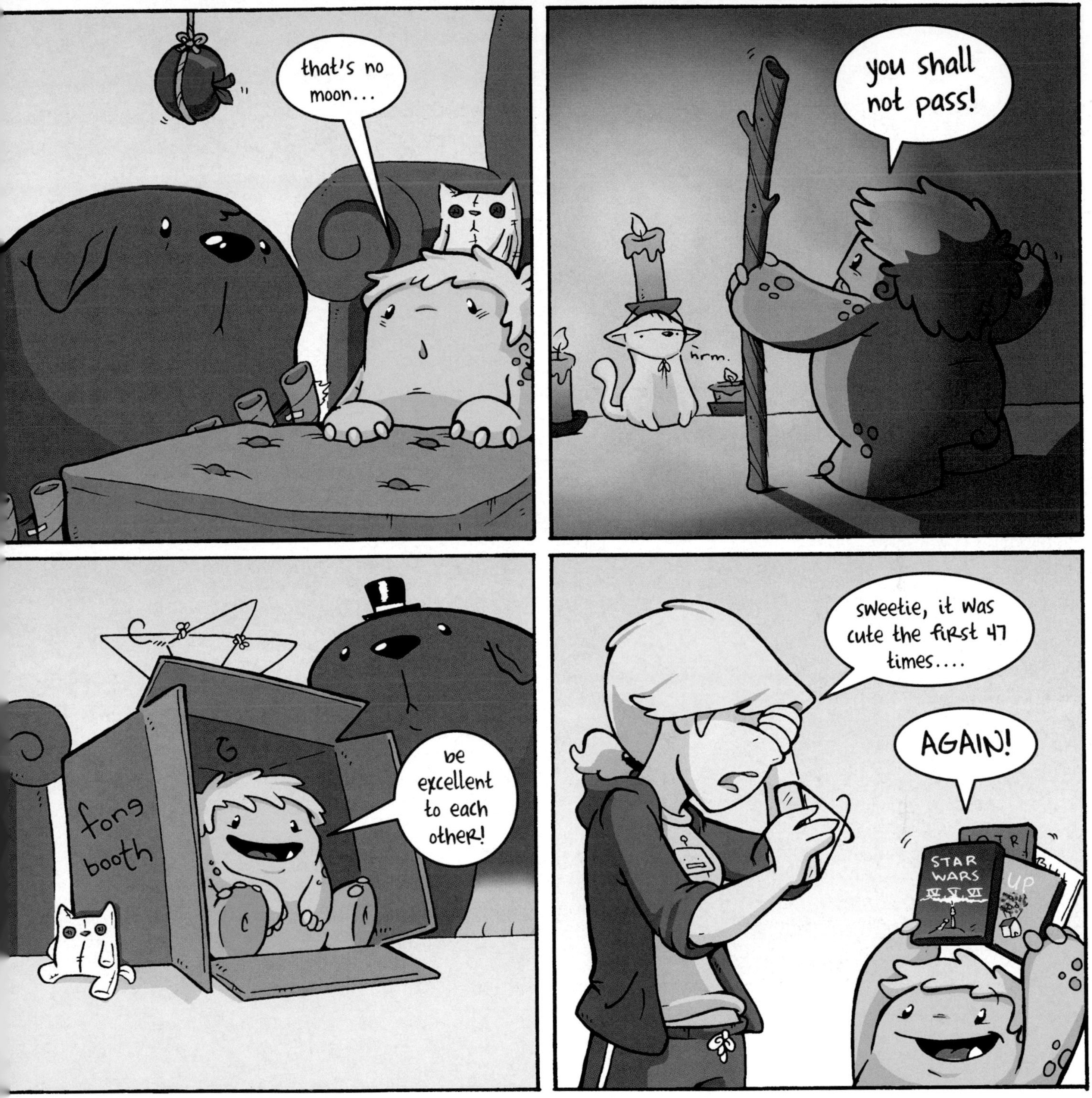
that's no moon...
you shall not pass!
hrm.
fong booth
be excellent to each other!
sweetie, it was cute the first 47 times....
AGAIN!
STAR WARS
UP

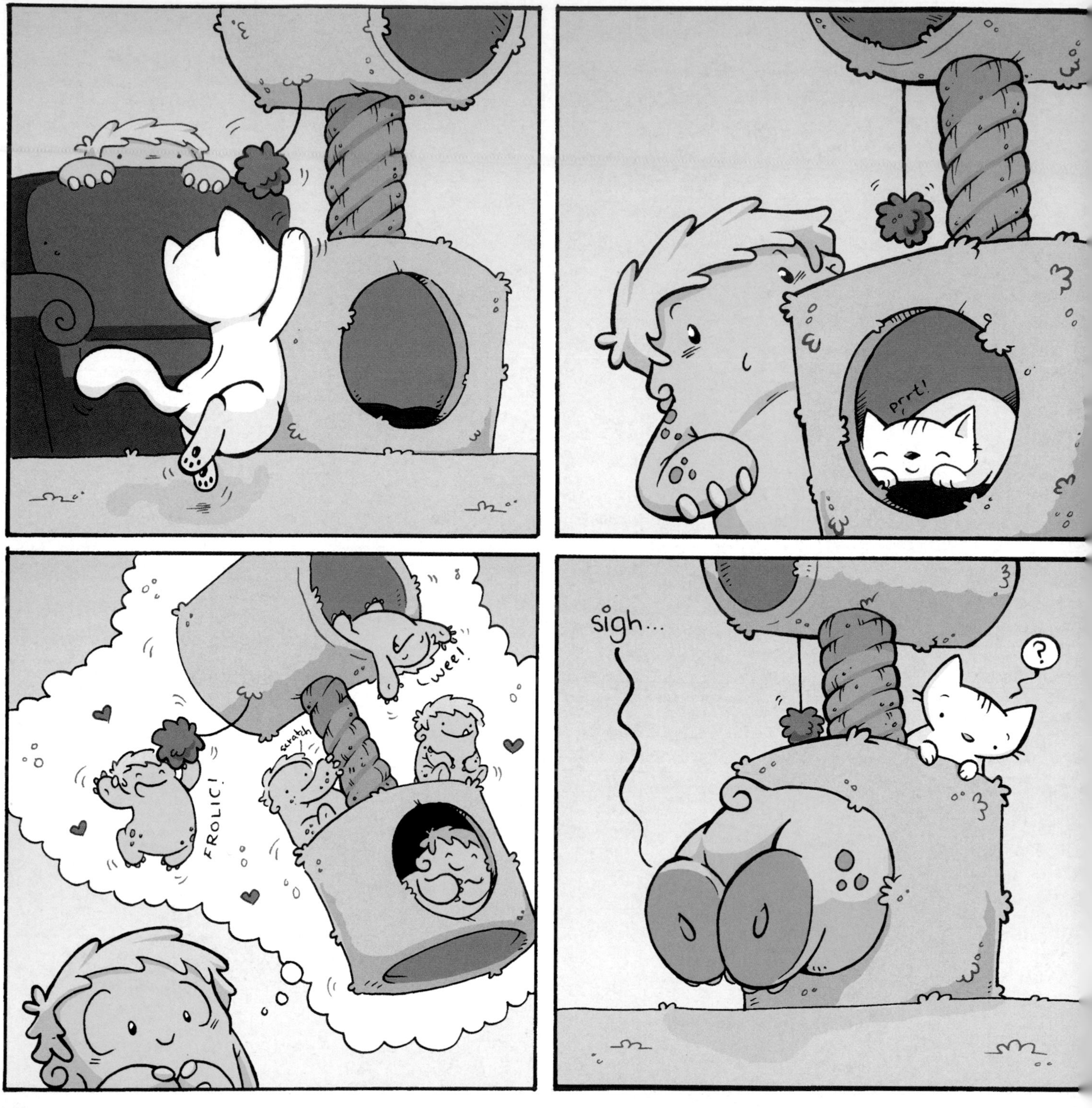
prrt!
Wee!
scratch
FROLIC!
sigh...
?

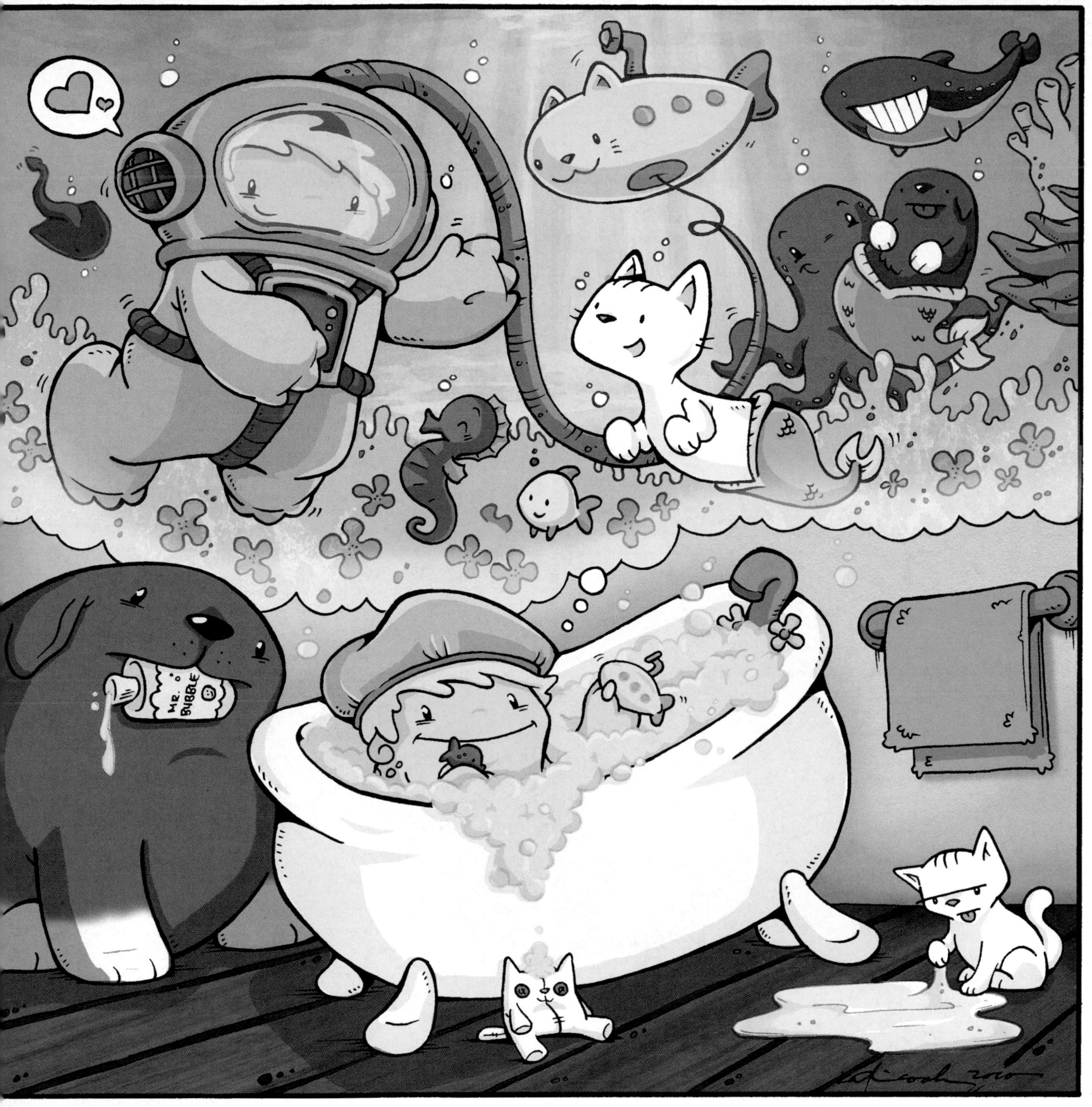
MR. BUBBLE

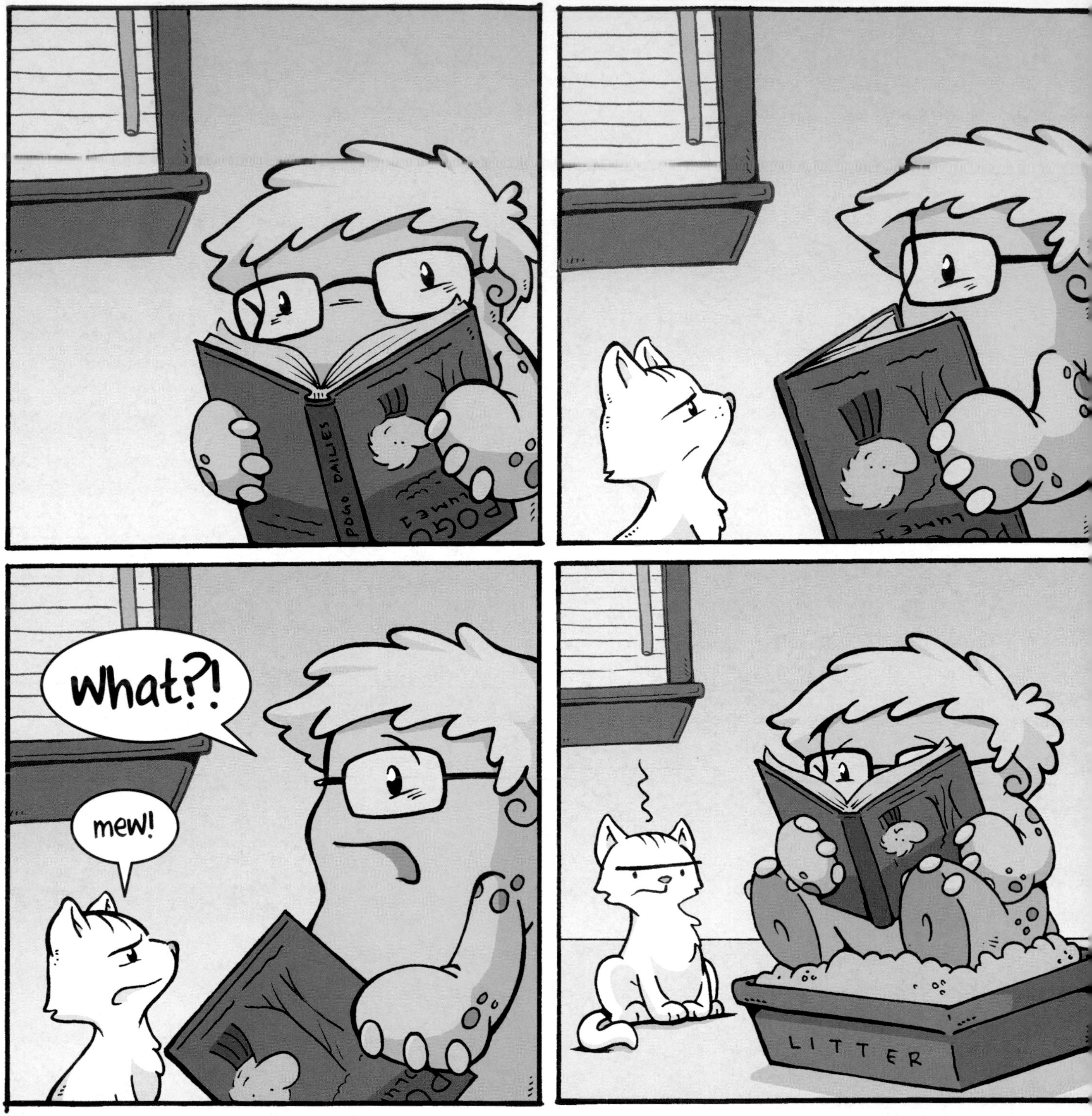
POGO DAILIES
What?!
mew!
LITTER

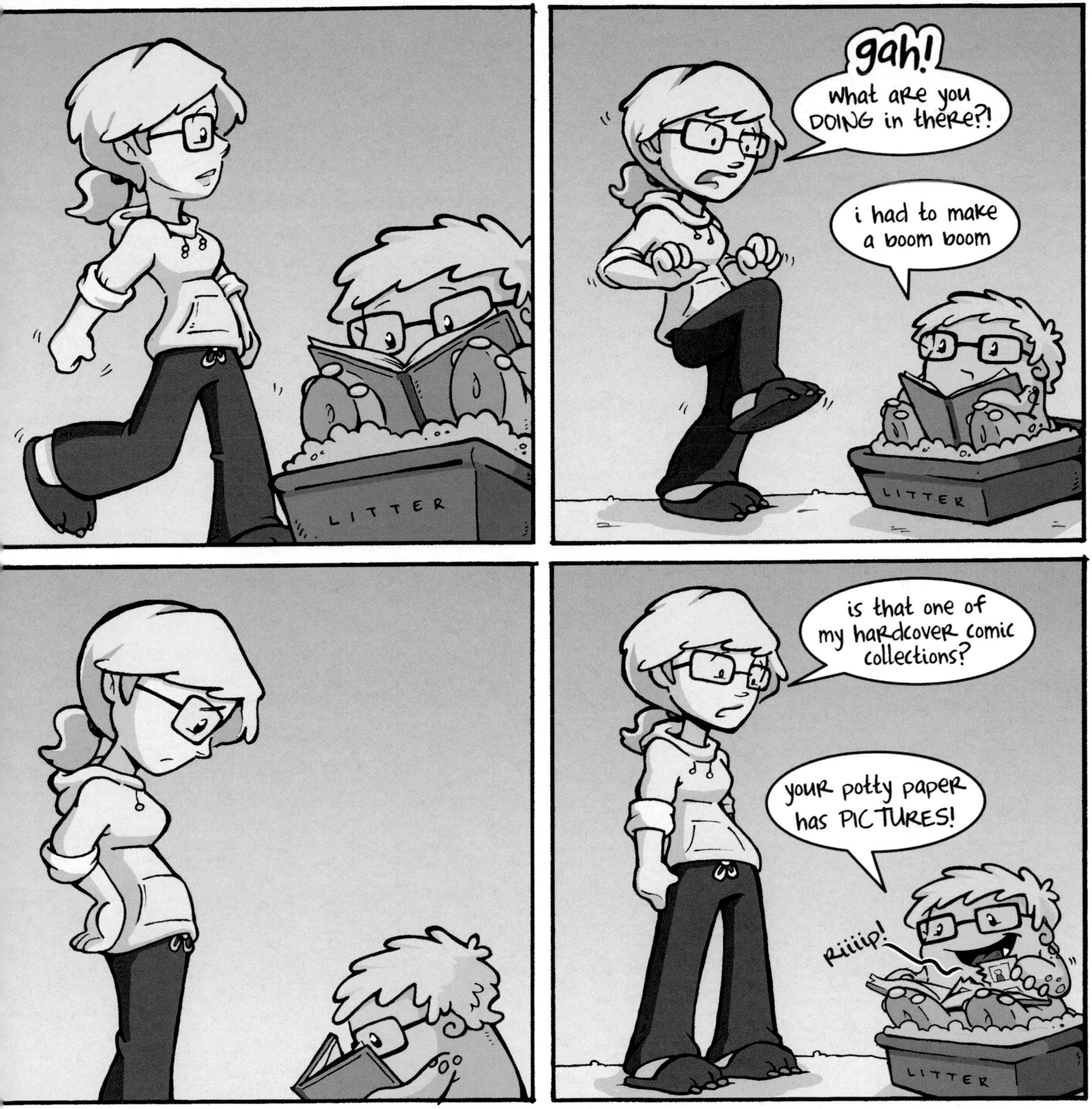
LITTER
gah!
what are you DOING in there?!
i had to make a boom boom
LITTER
is that one of my hardcover comic collections?
your potty paper has PICTURES!
Riiiip!
LITTER

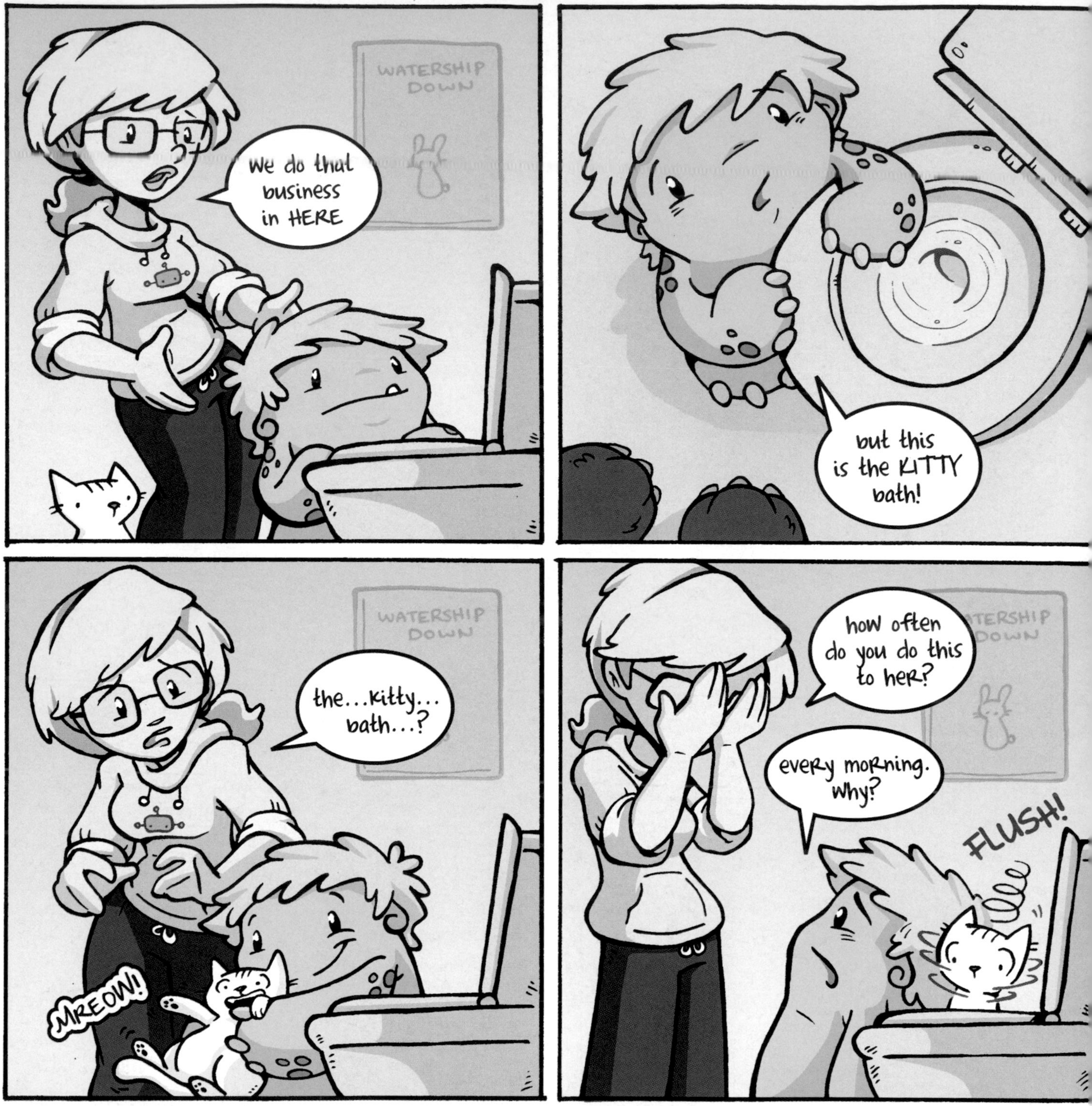

WATERSHIP DOWN
we do that business in HERE
but this is the KITTY bath!
WATERSHIP DOWN
the...kitty... bath...?
MREOW!
how often do you do this to her?
every morning. why?
FLUSH!

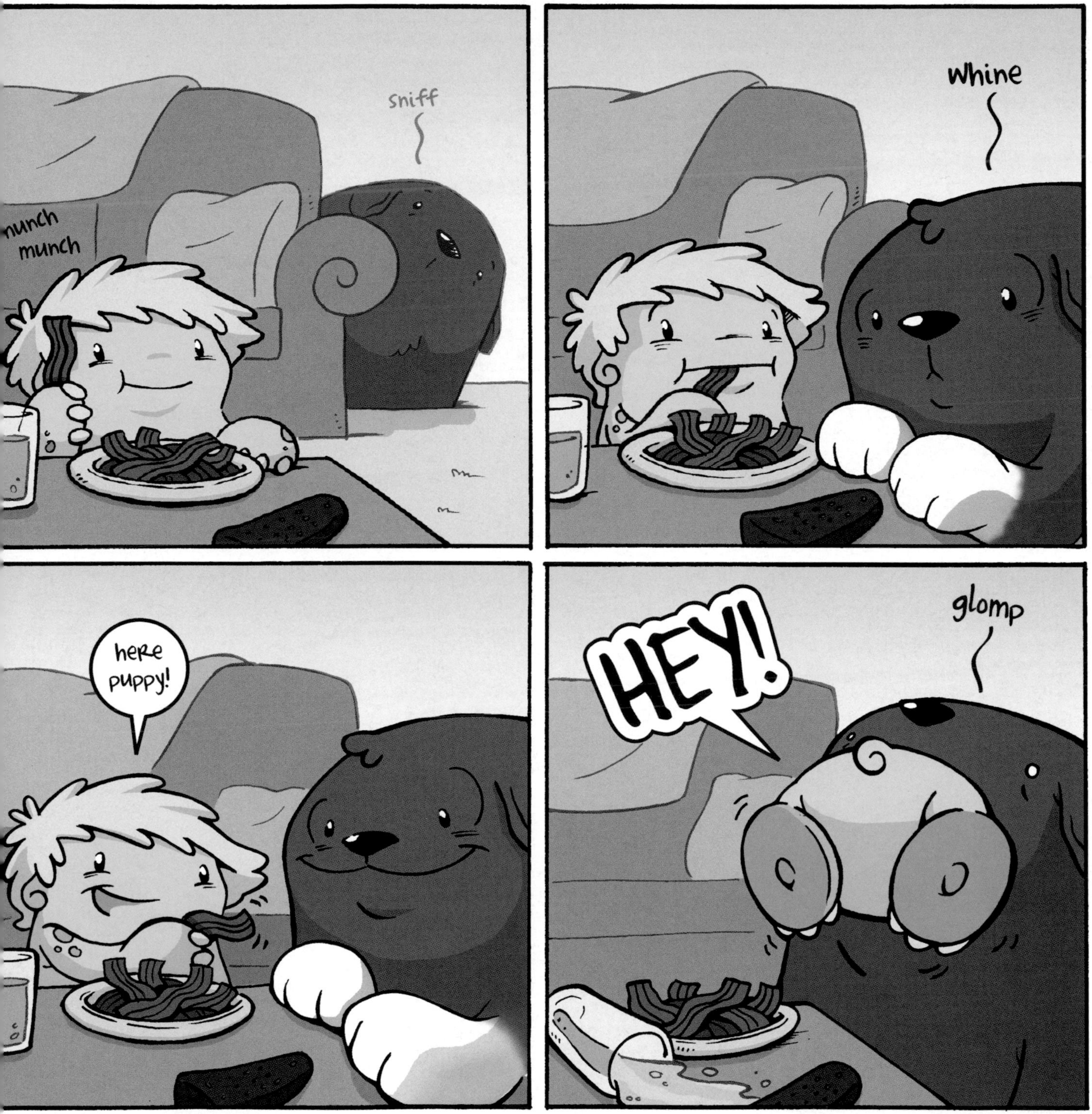
munch
munch
sniff
whine
here puppy!
HEY!
glomp

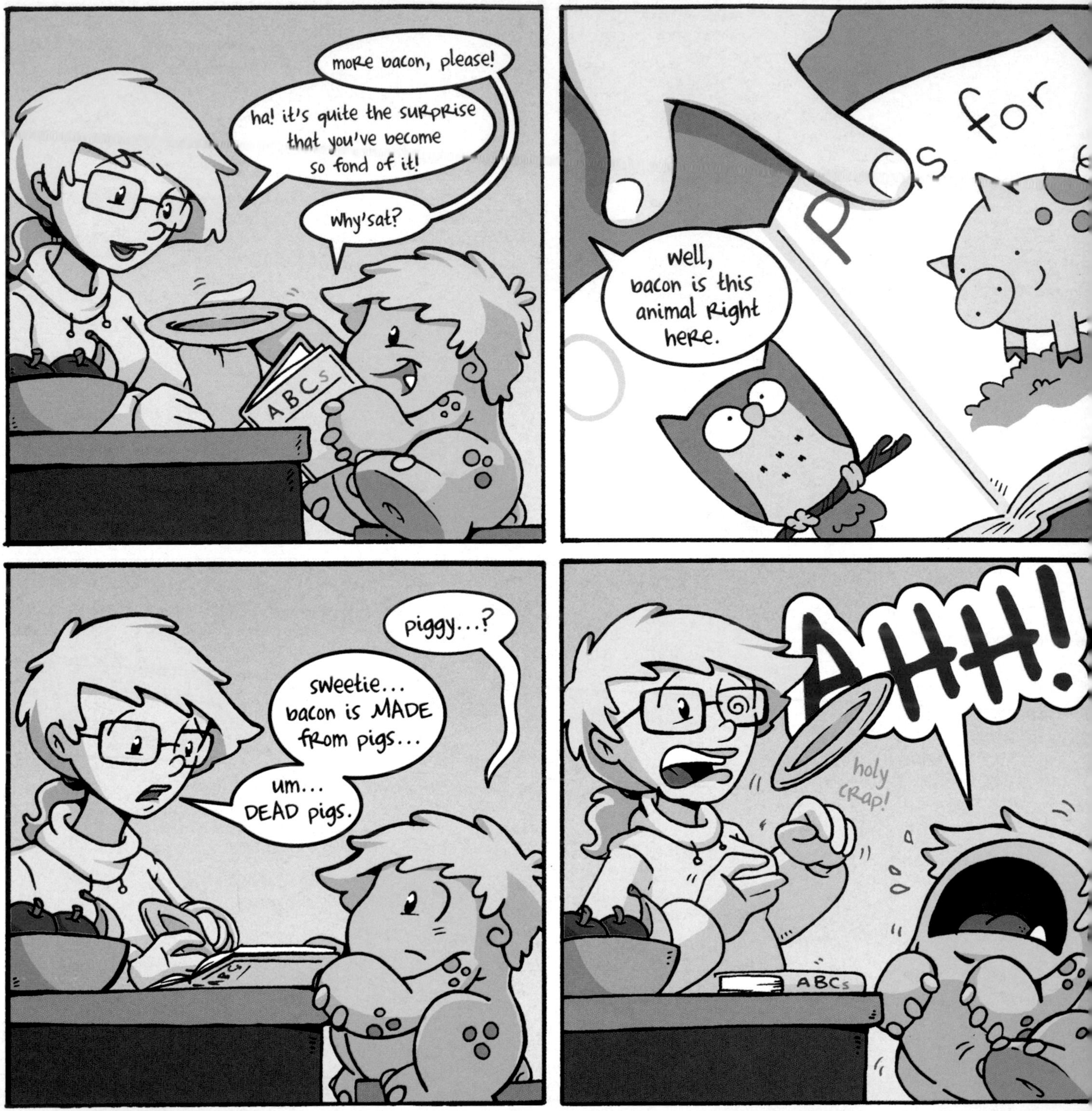
more bacon, please!
ha! it's quite the surprise that you've become so fond of it!
Why'sat?
ABCs
P is for
Well, bacon is this animal right here.
piggy...?
sweetie... bacon is MADE from pigs...
um... DEAD pigs.
ABC
AHH!
holy crap!
ABCs

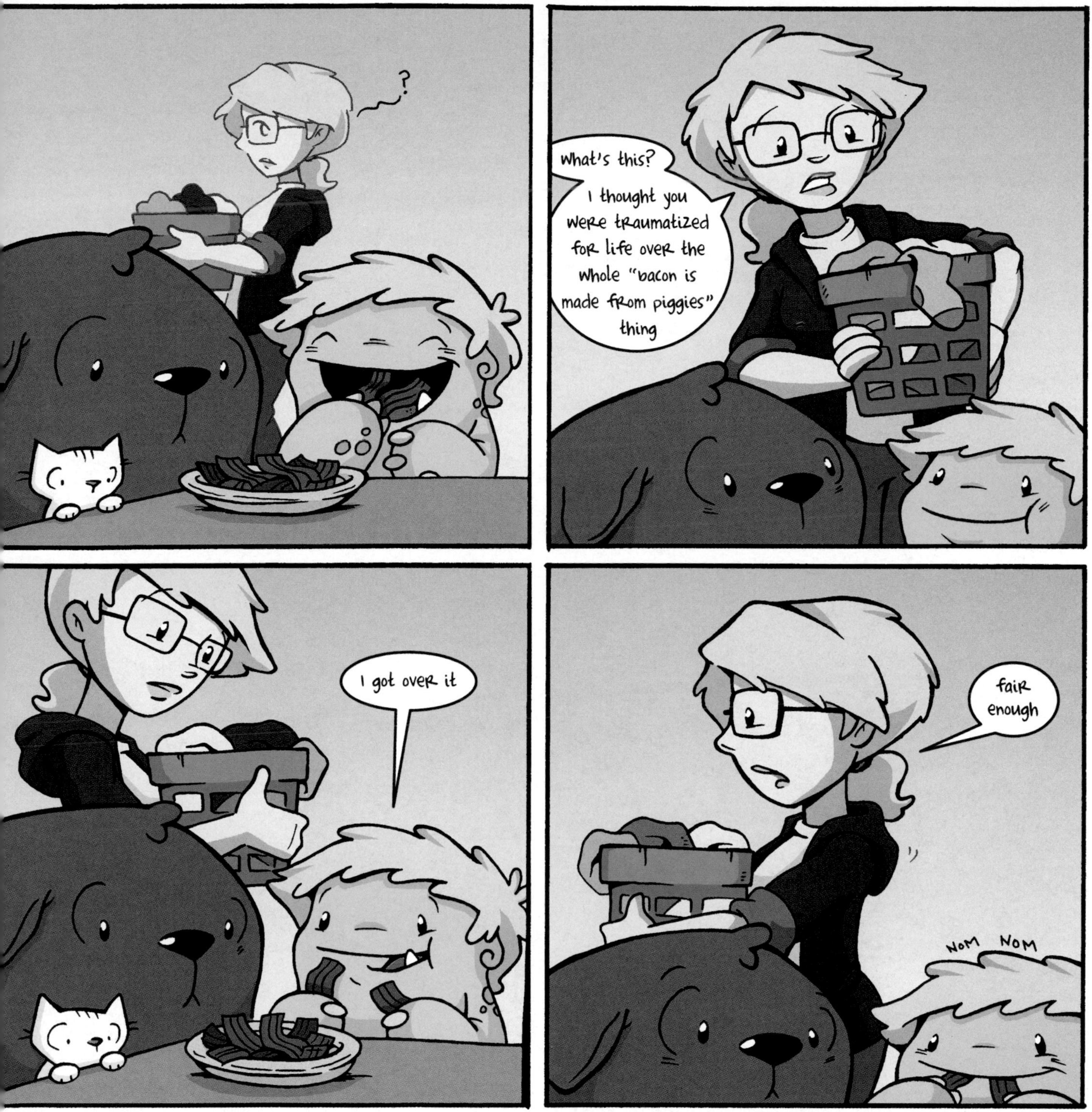
?
What's this?
I thought you were traumatized for life over the whole "bacon is made from piggies" thing
I got over it
fair enough
NOM NOM

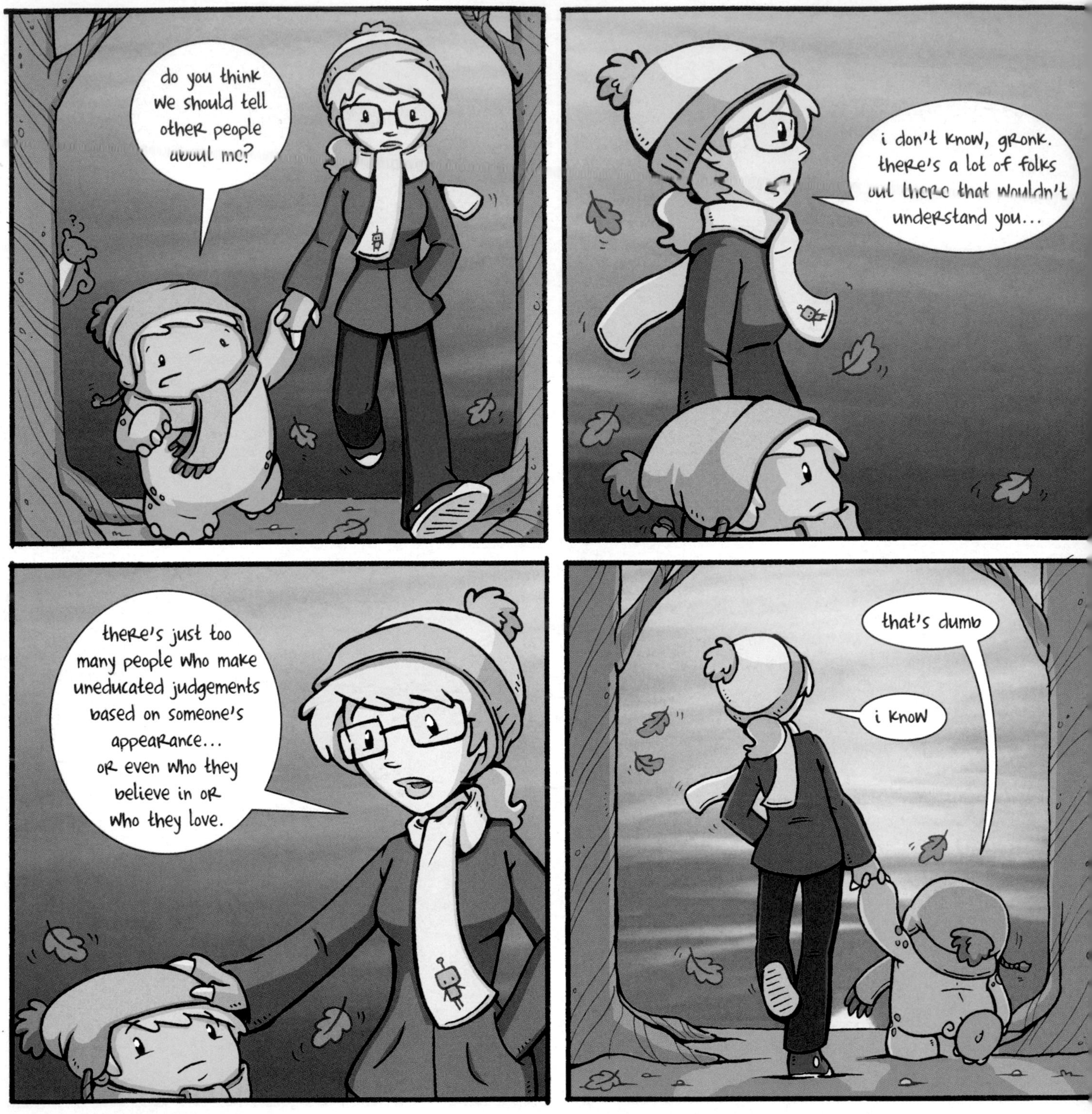
do you think we should tell other people about me?
i don't know, gronk. there's a lot of folks out there that wouldn't understand you...
there's just too many people who make uneducated judgements based on someone's appearance... or even who they believe in or who they love.
that's dumb
i know

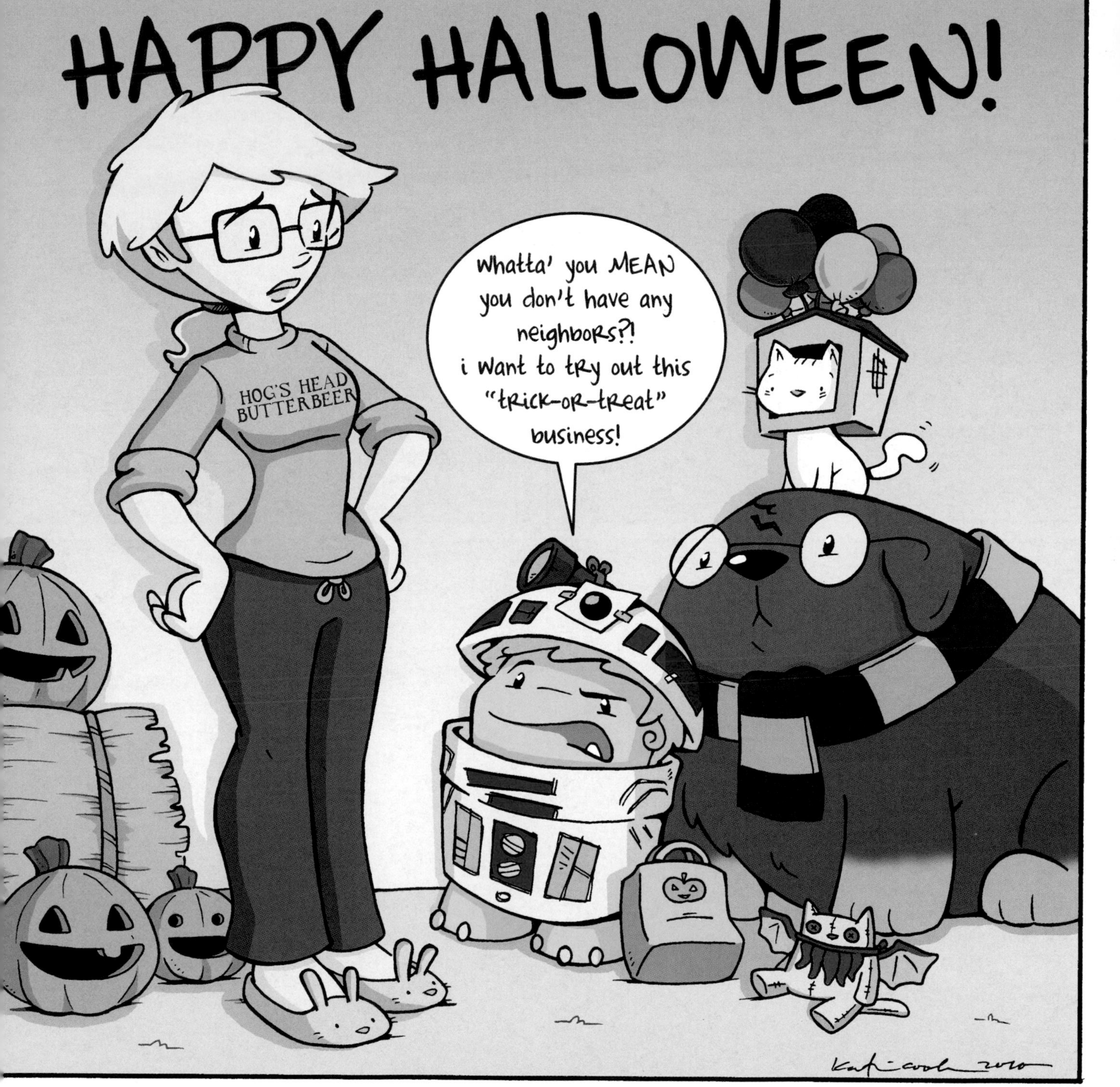
HAPPY HALLOWEEN!
HOG'S HEAD BUTTERBEER
Whatta' you MEAN you don't have any neighbors?! i want to try out this "trick-or-treat" business!

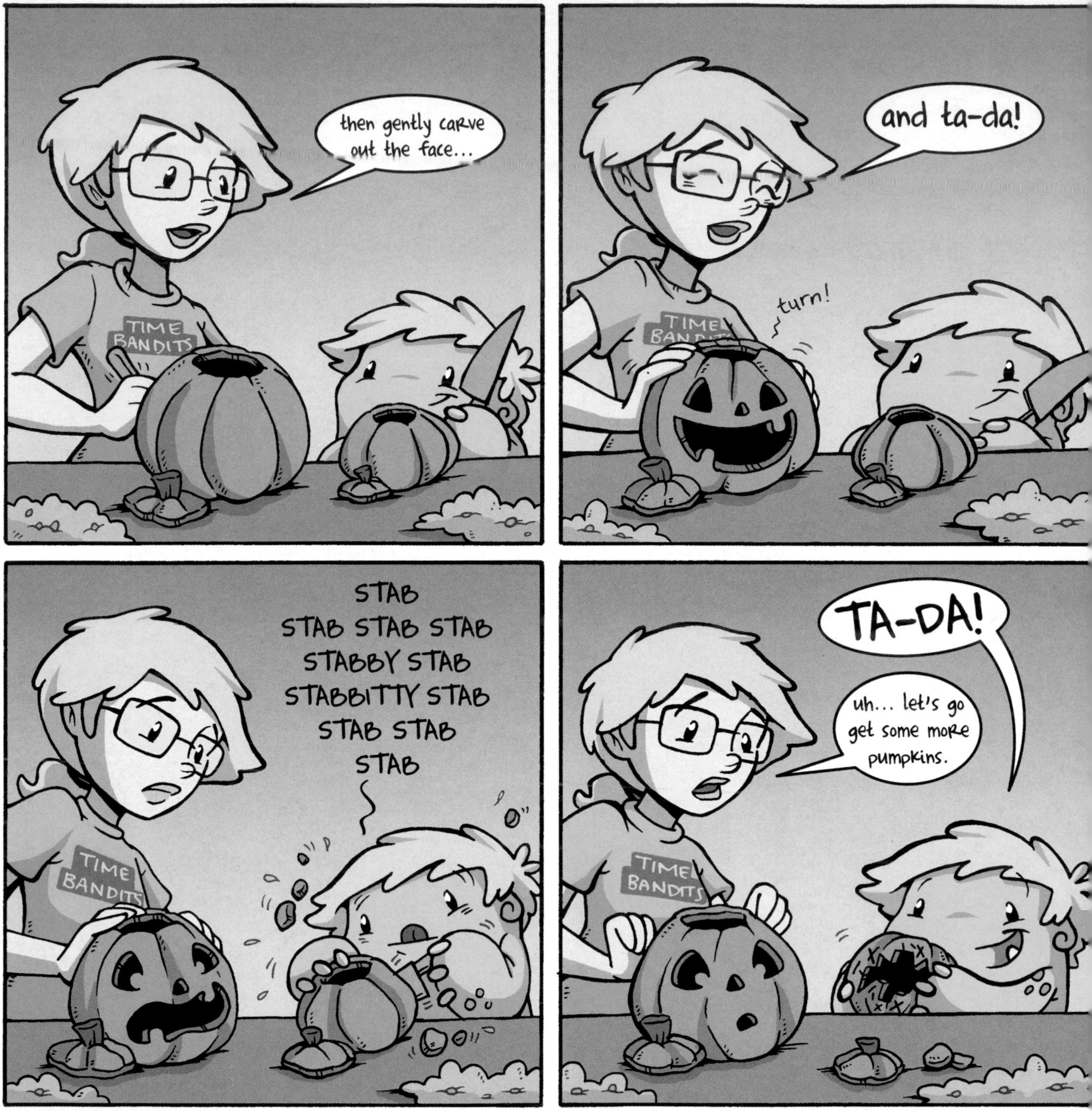
then gently carve out the face...
and ta-da!
turn!
TIME BANDITS
STAB
STAB STAB STAB
STABBY STAB
STABBITTY STAB
STAB STAB
STAB
TA-DA!
uh... let's go get some more pumpkins.

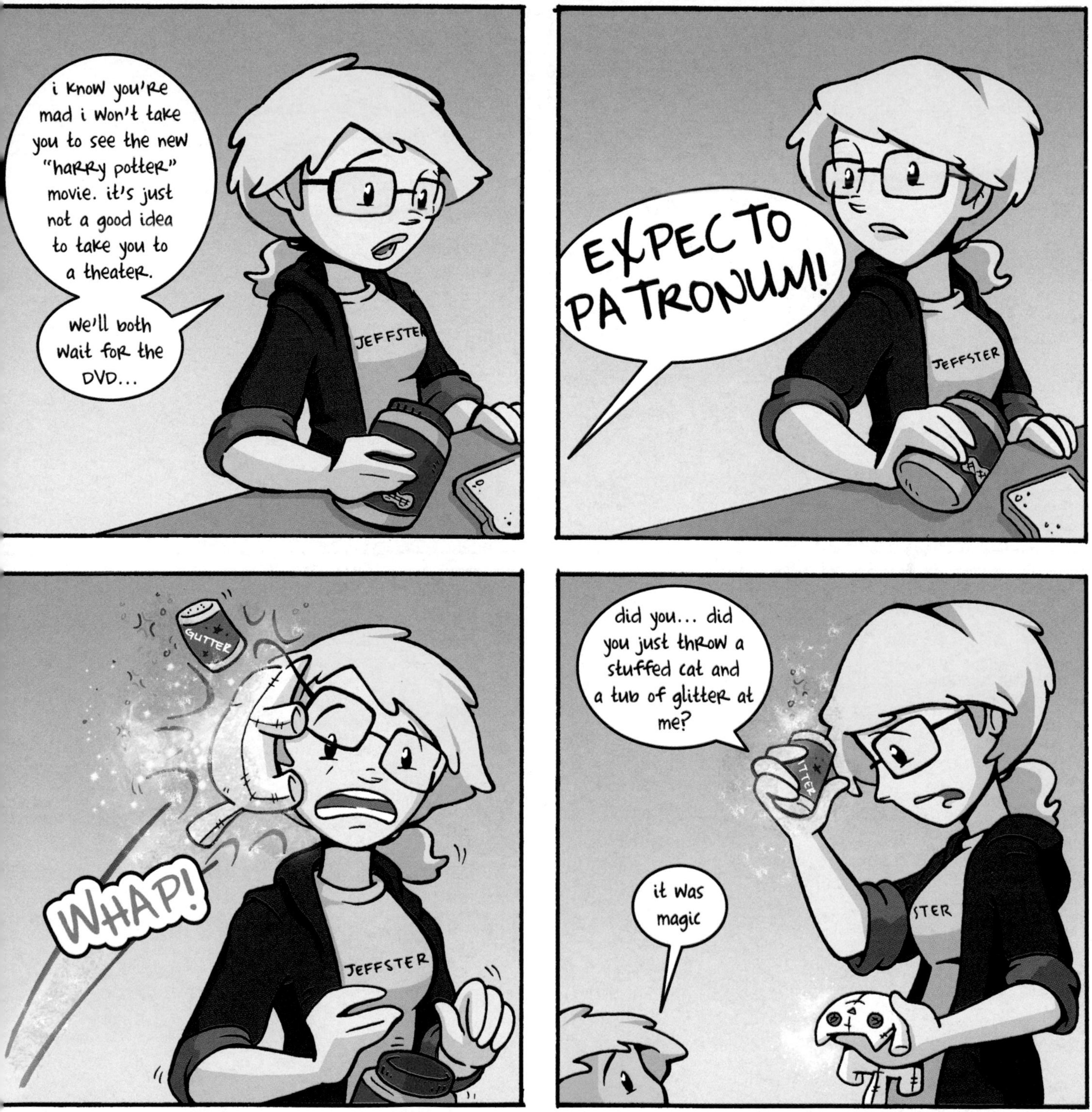
i know you're mad i won't take you to see the new "harry potter" movie. it's just not a good idea to take you to a theater.
we'll both wait for the DVD...
JEFFSTER
EXPECTO PATRONUM!
JEFFSTER
GLITTER
WHAP!
JEFFSTER
did you... did you just throw a stuffed cat and a tub of glitter at me?
it was magic
STER

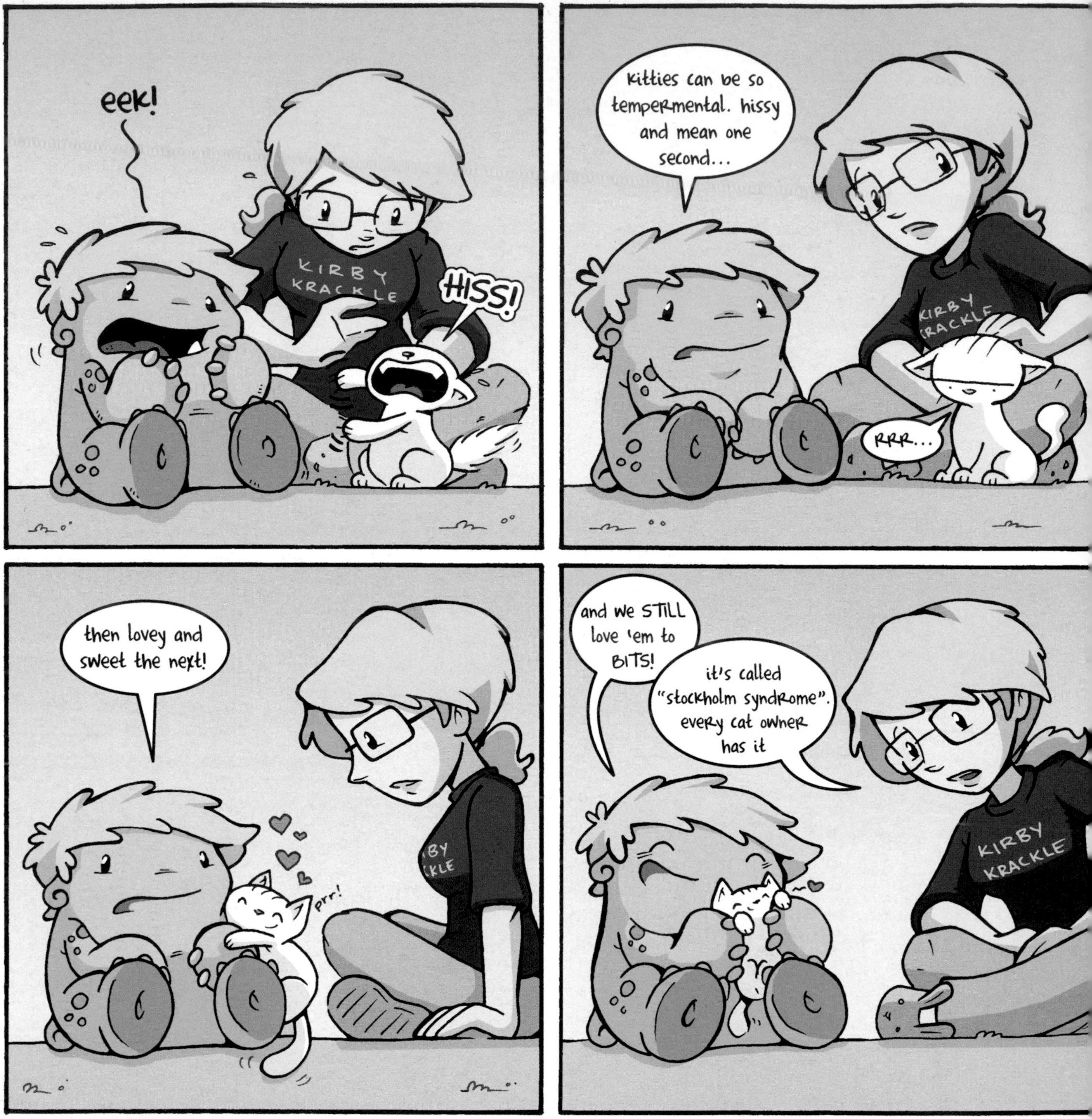
eek!
HISS!
KIRBY KRACKLE
kitties can be so tempermental. hissy and mean one second...
RRR...
then lovey and sweet the next!
prr!
and we STILL love 'em to BITS!
it's called "stockholm syndrome". every cat owner has it

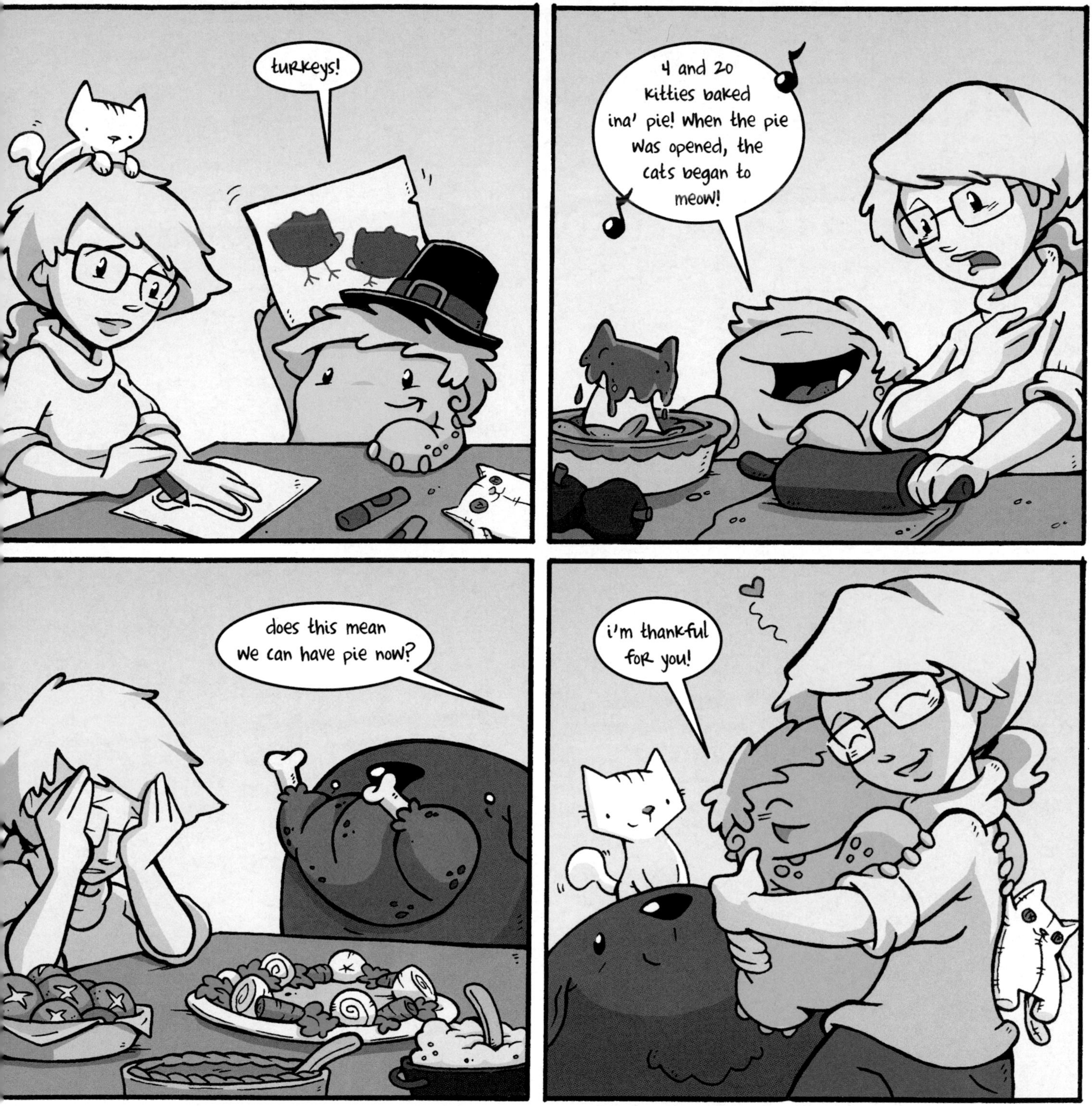
turkeys!
4 and 20 kitties baked ina' pie! When the pie was opened, the cats began to meow!
does this mean we can have pie now?
i'm thankful for you!

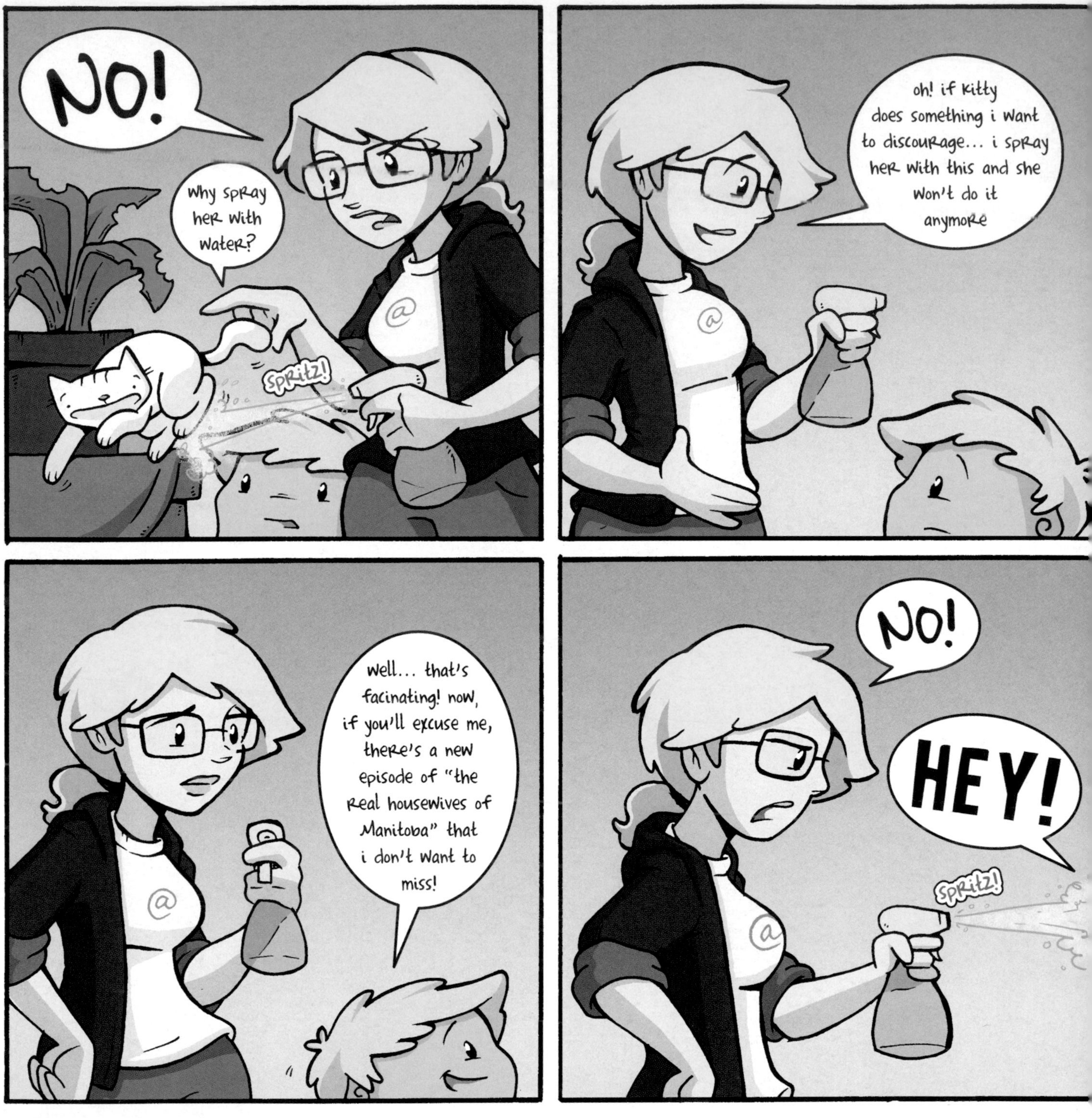
NO!
Why spray her with water?
SPRITZ!
oh! if kitty does something i want to discourage... i spray her with this and she won't do it anymore
well... that's facinating! now, if you'll excuse me, there's a new episode of "the real housewives of Manitoba" that i don't want to miss!
NO!
HEY!
SPRITZ!

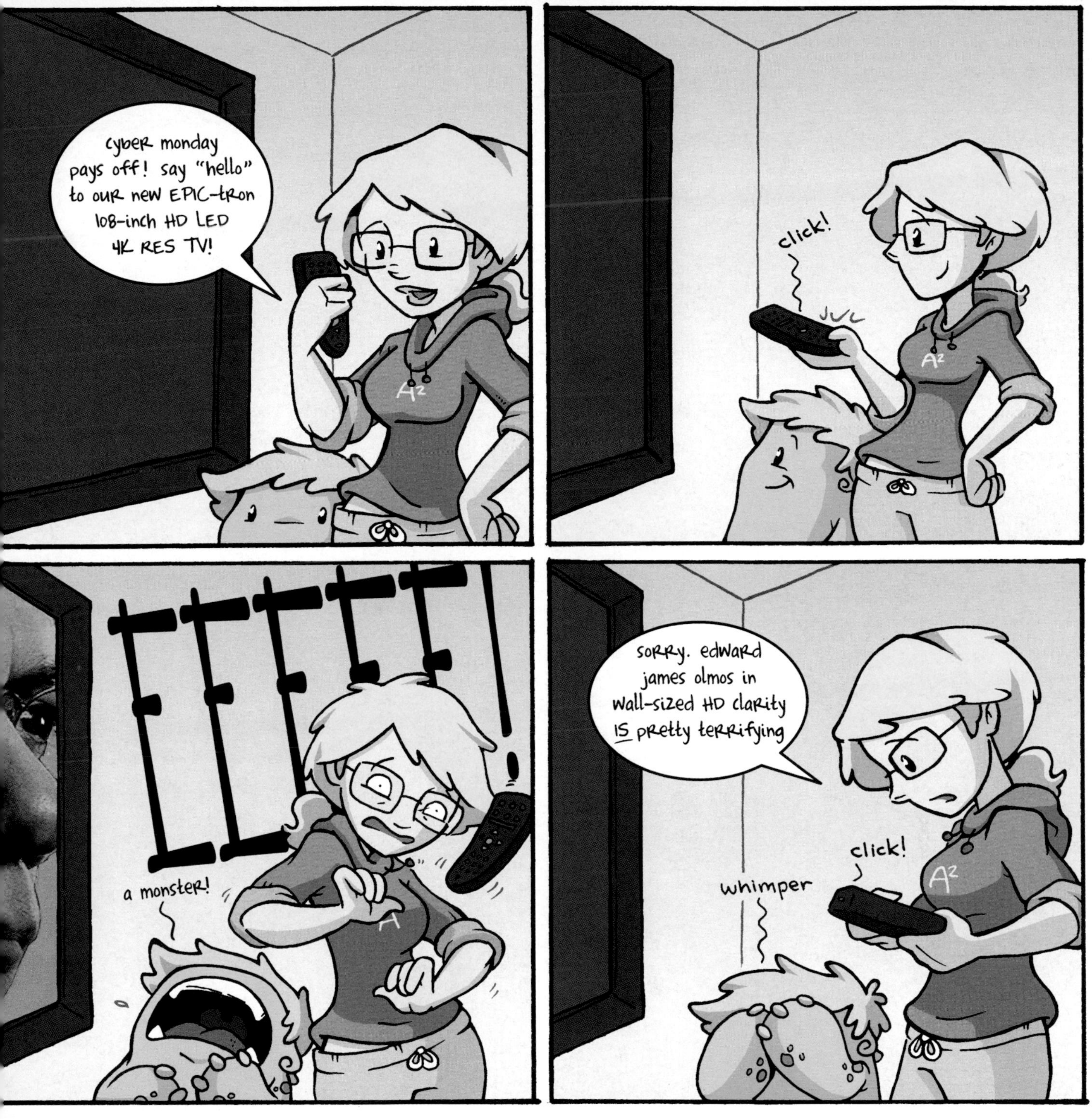
cyber monday pays off! say "hello" to our new EPIC-tron 108-inch HD LED 4K RES TV!
click!
EEEEE!
a monster!
sorry. edward james olmos in wall-sized HD clarity IS pretty terrifying
whimper
click!

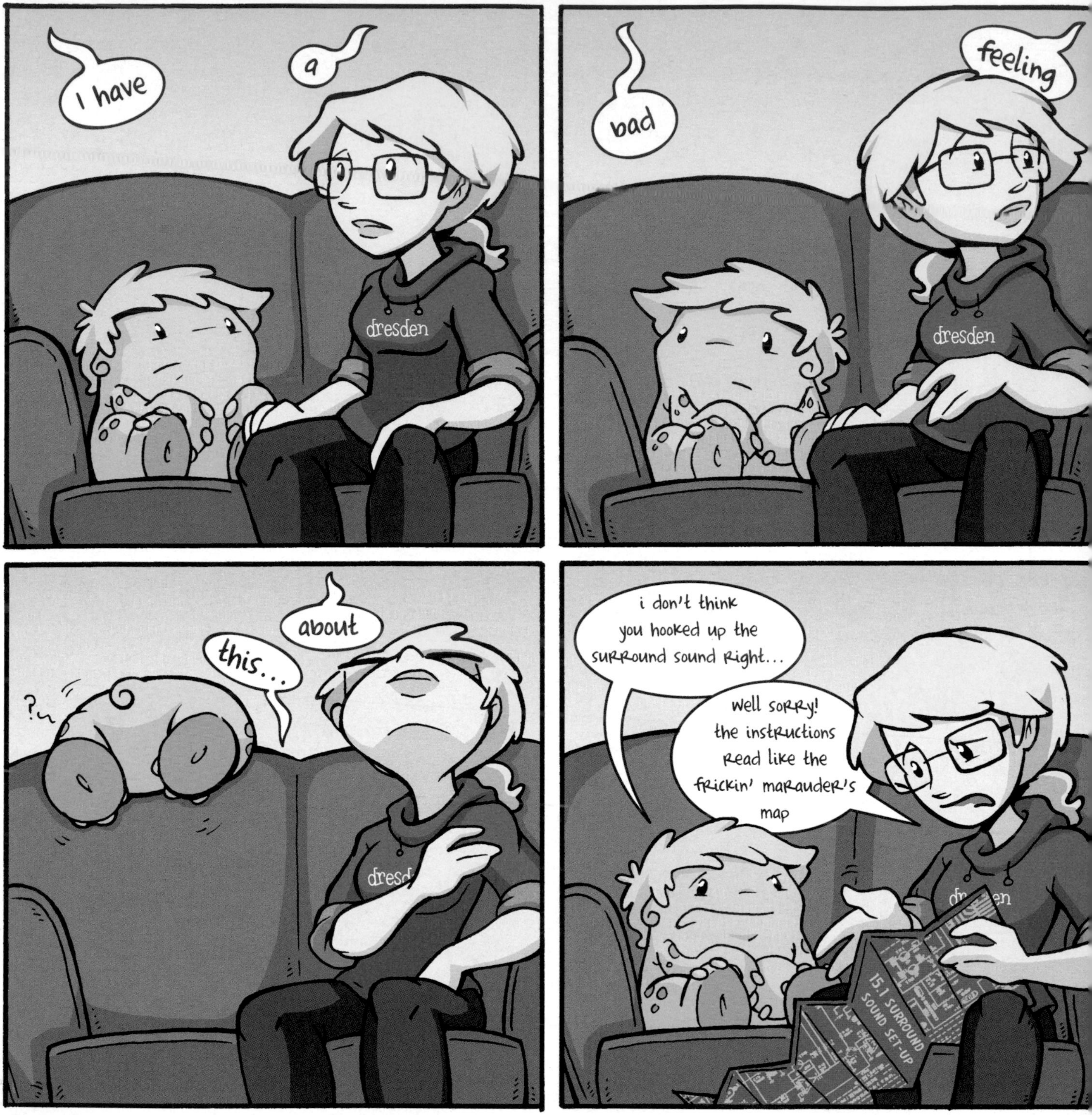
I have
a
bad
feeling
dresden
about
this...
?~
i don't think you hooked up the surround sound right...
well sorry! the instructions read like the frickin' marauder's map
15.1 SURROUND SOUND SET-UP

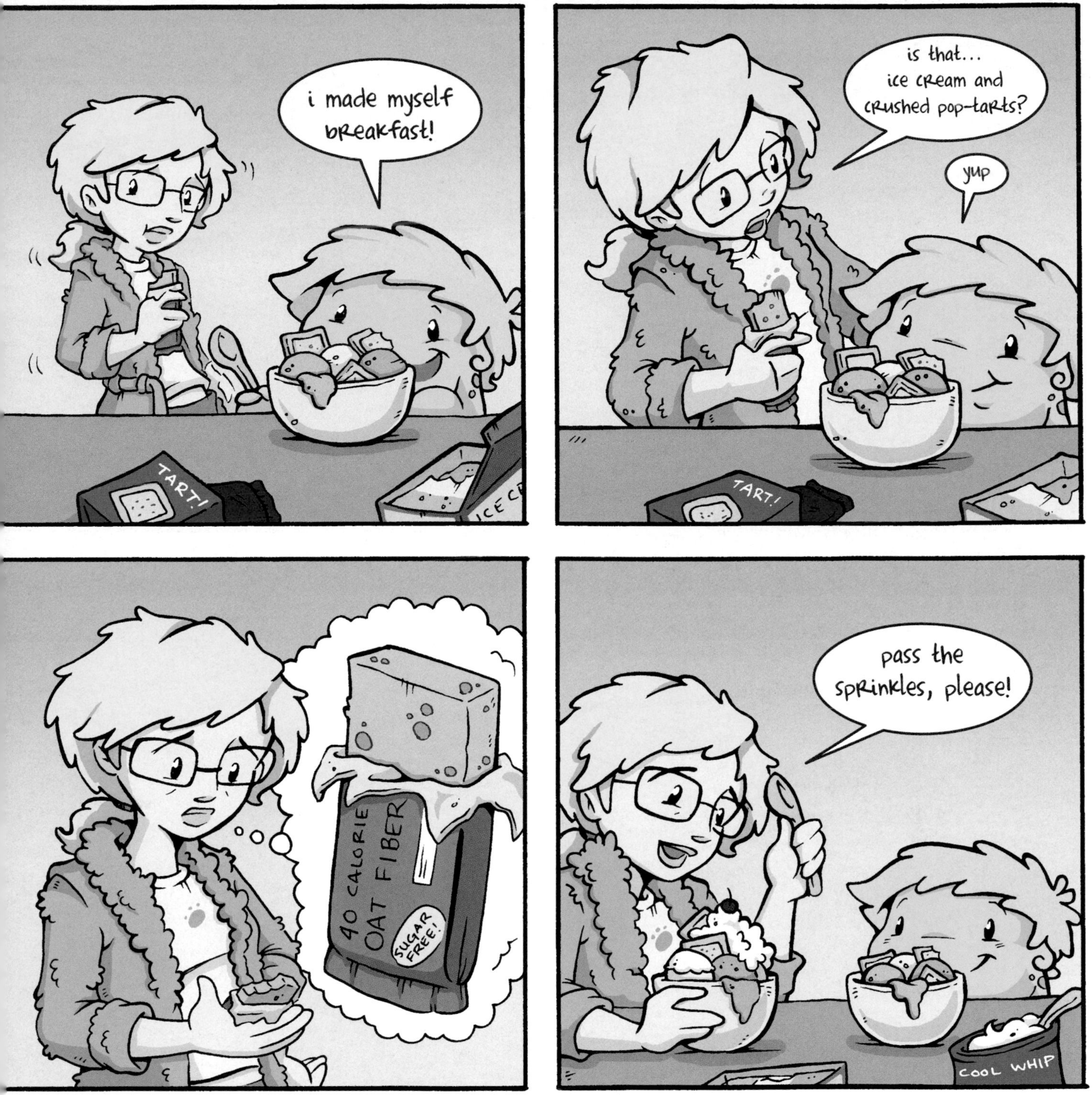
i made myself breakfast!
TART!
ICE CR
is that... ice cream and crushed pop-tarts?
yup
TART!
40 CALORIE OAT FIBER
SUGAR FREE!
pass the sprinkles, please!
COOL WHIP

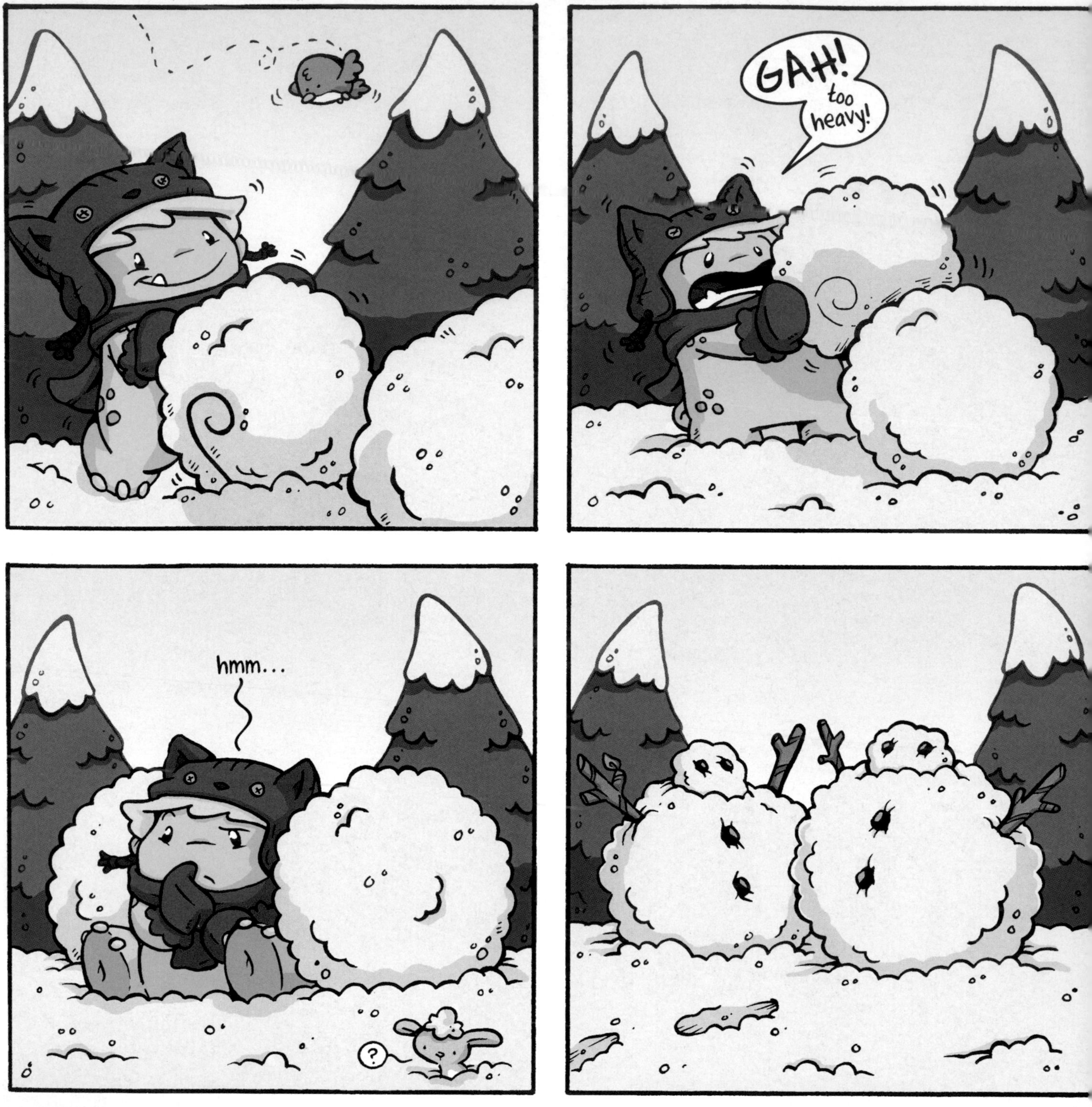
GAH! too heavy!
hmm...
?

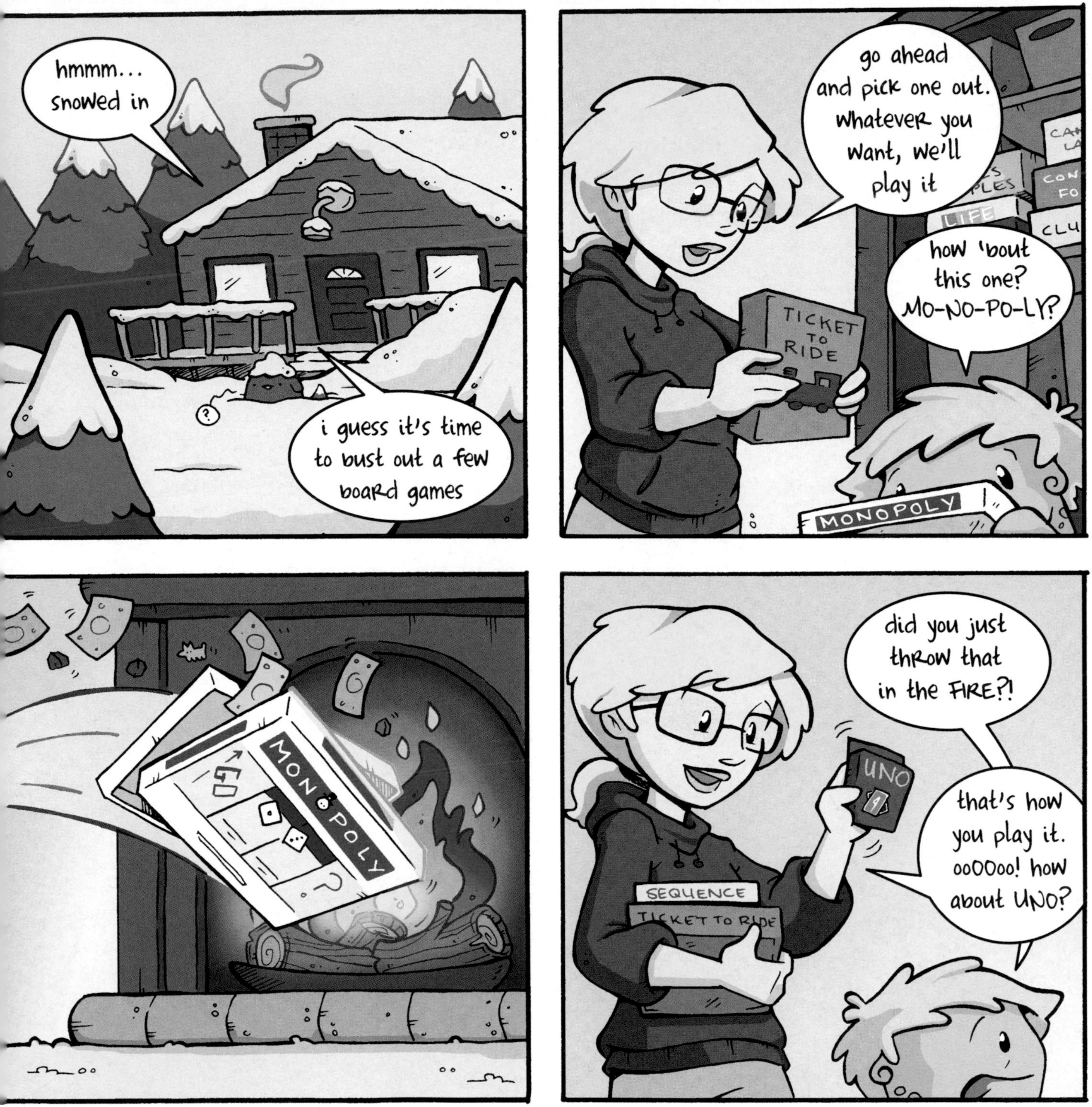
hmmm... snowed in
i guess it's time to bust out a few board games
go ahead and pick one out. whatever you want, we'll play it
TICKET TO RIDE
LIFE
how 'bout this one? MO-NO-PO-LY?
MONOPOLY
MONOPOLY
GO
did you just throw that in the FIRE?!
UNO
SEQUENCE
TICKET TO RIDE
that's how you play it. oooOoo! how about UNO?

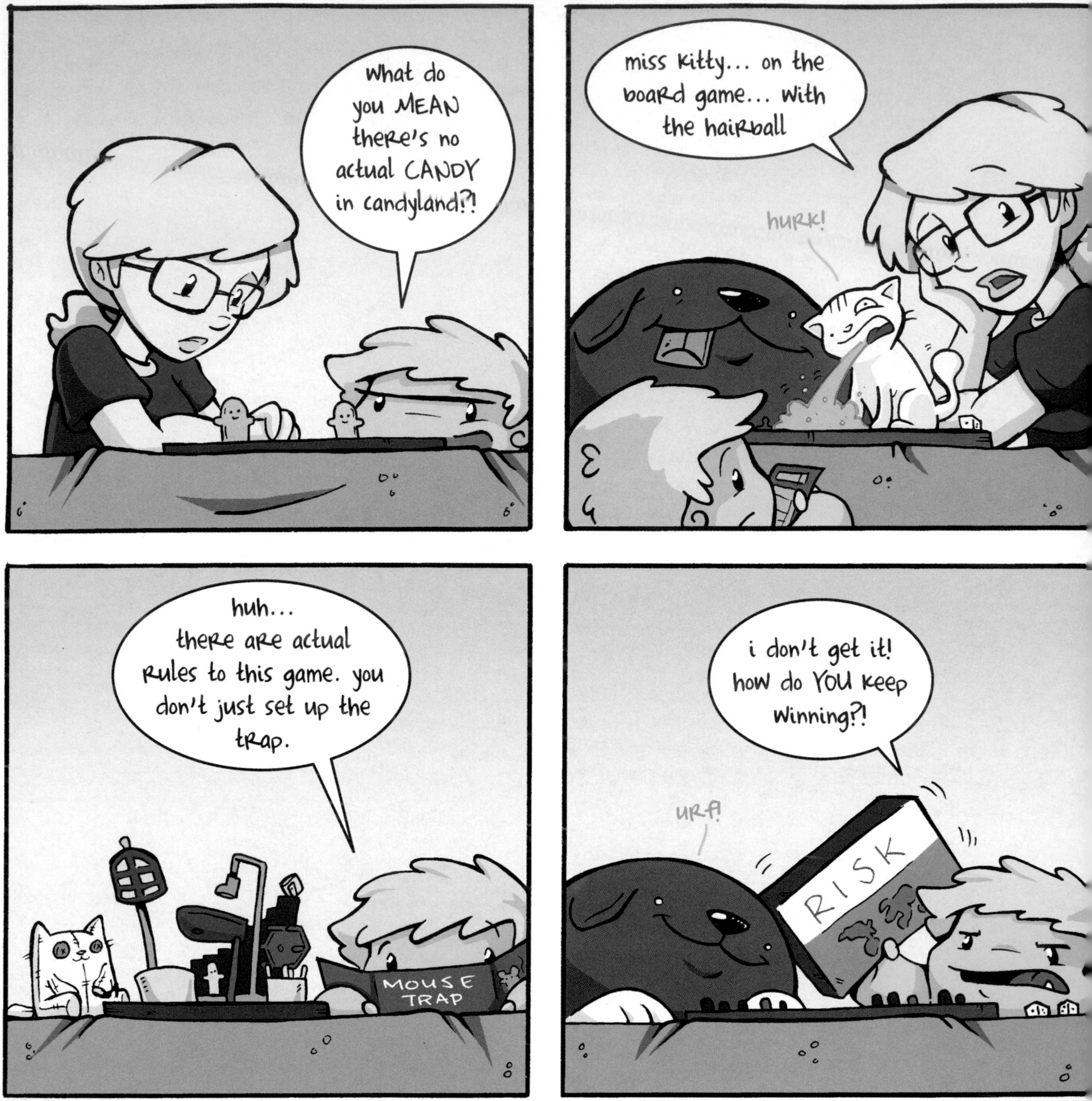
What do you MEAN there's no actual CANDY in candyland?!
miss kitty... on the board game... with the hairball
hurk!
huh... there are actual rules to this game. you don't just set up the trap.
MOUSE TRAP
i don't get it! how do YOU keep winning?!
URF!
RISK

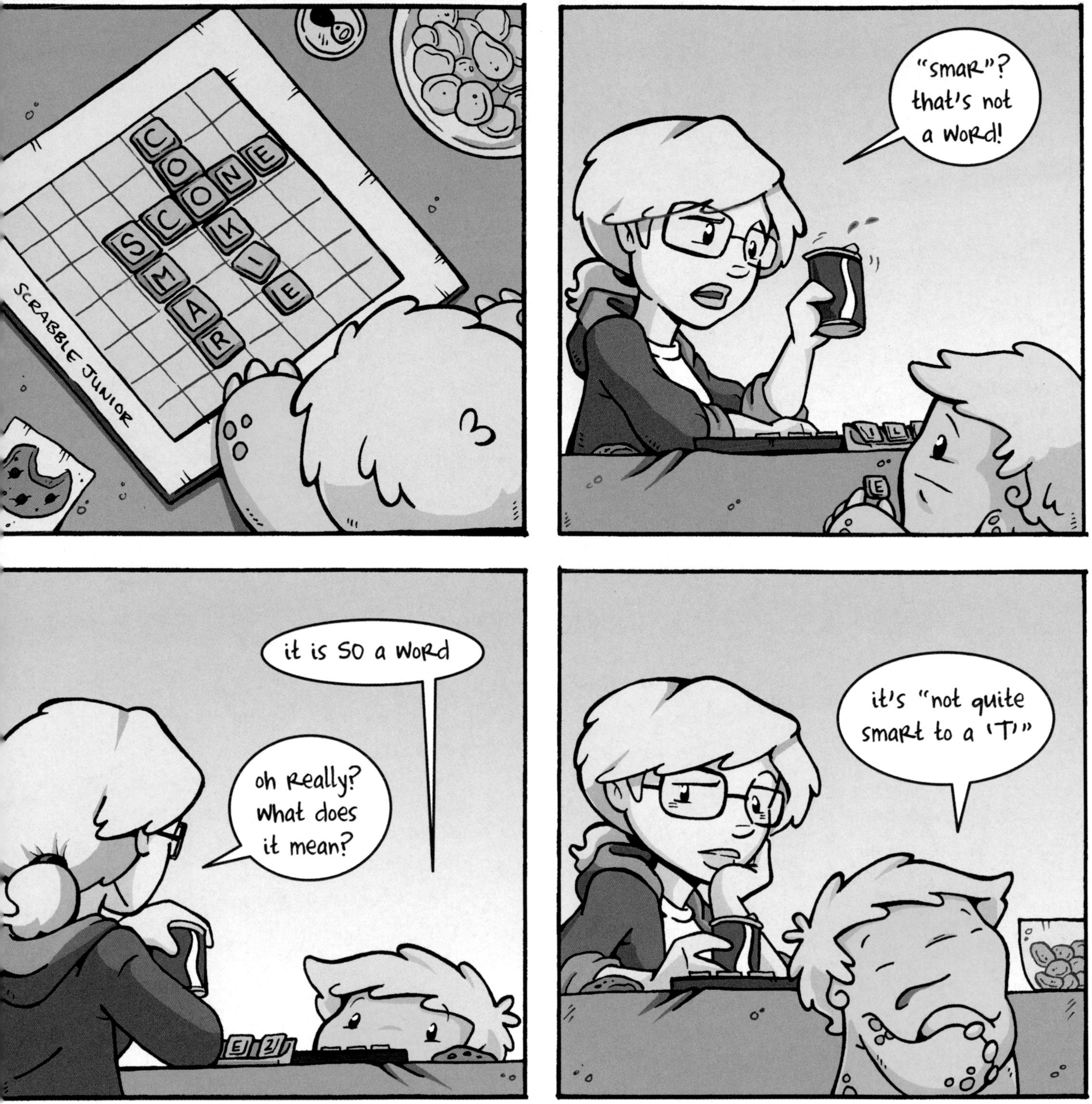
COOKIE
CONE
SMAR
SCRABBLE JUNIOR
"smar"? that's not a word!
it is SO a word
oh really? what does it mean?
it's "not quite smart to a 'T'"

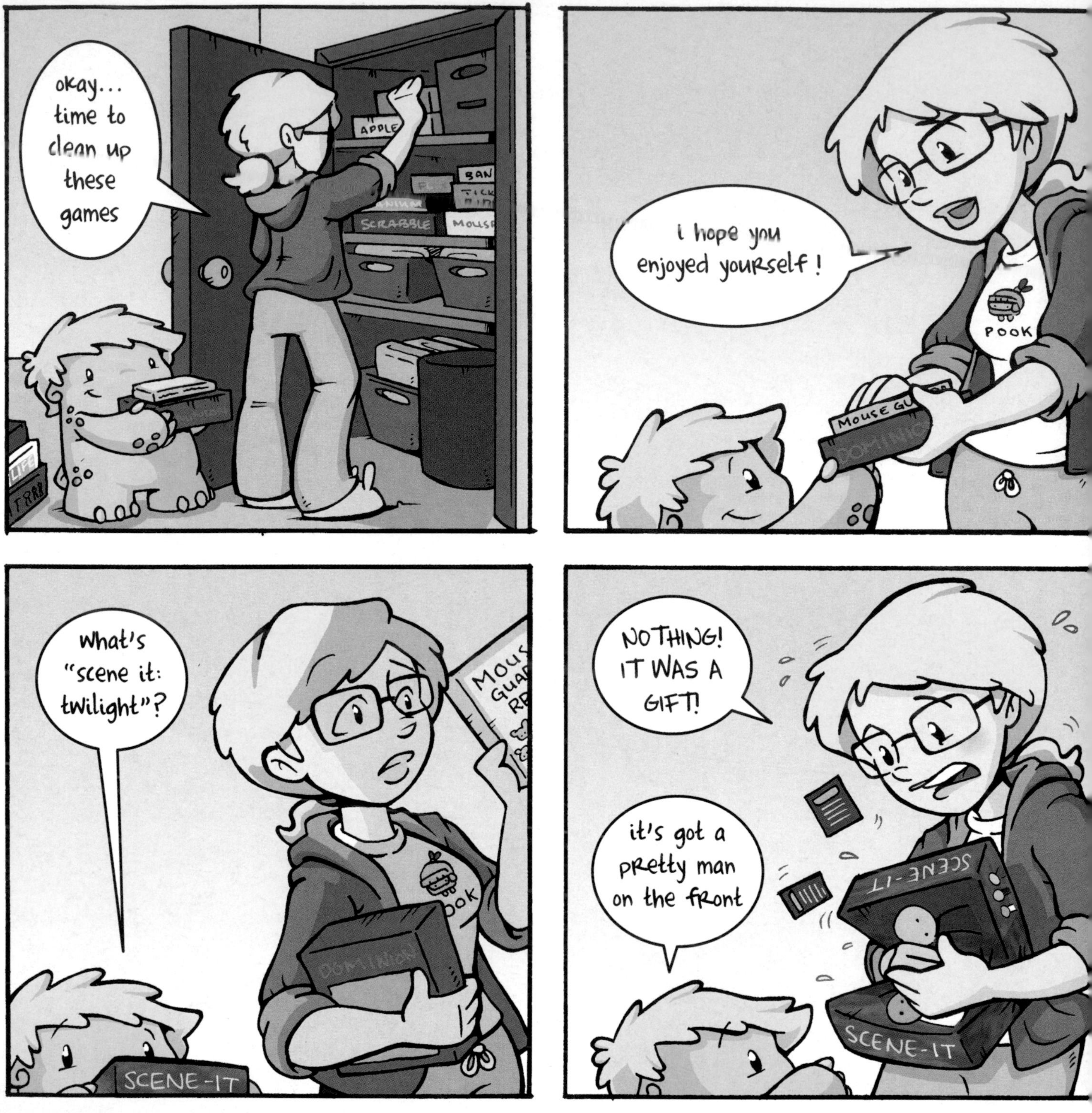
okay... time to clean up these games
APPLE
BAN
SCRABBLE
LIFE
i hope you enjoyed yourself!
POOK
MOUSE GU
DOMINIO
What's "scene it: twilight"?
MOUS GUAR RP
DOMINION
SCENE-IT
NOTHING! IT WAS A GIFT!
it's got a pretty man on the front
SCENE-IT
SCENE-IT

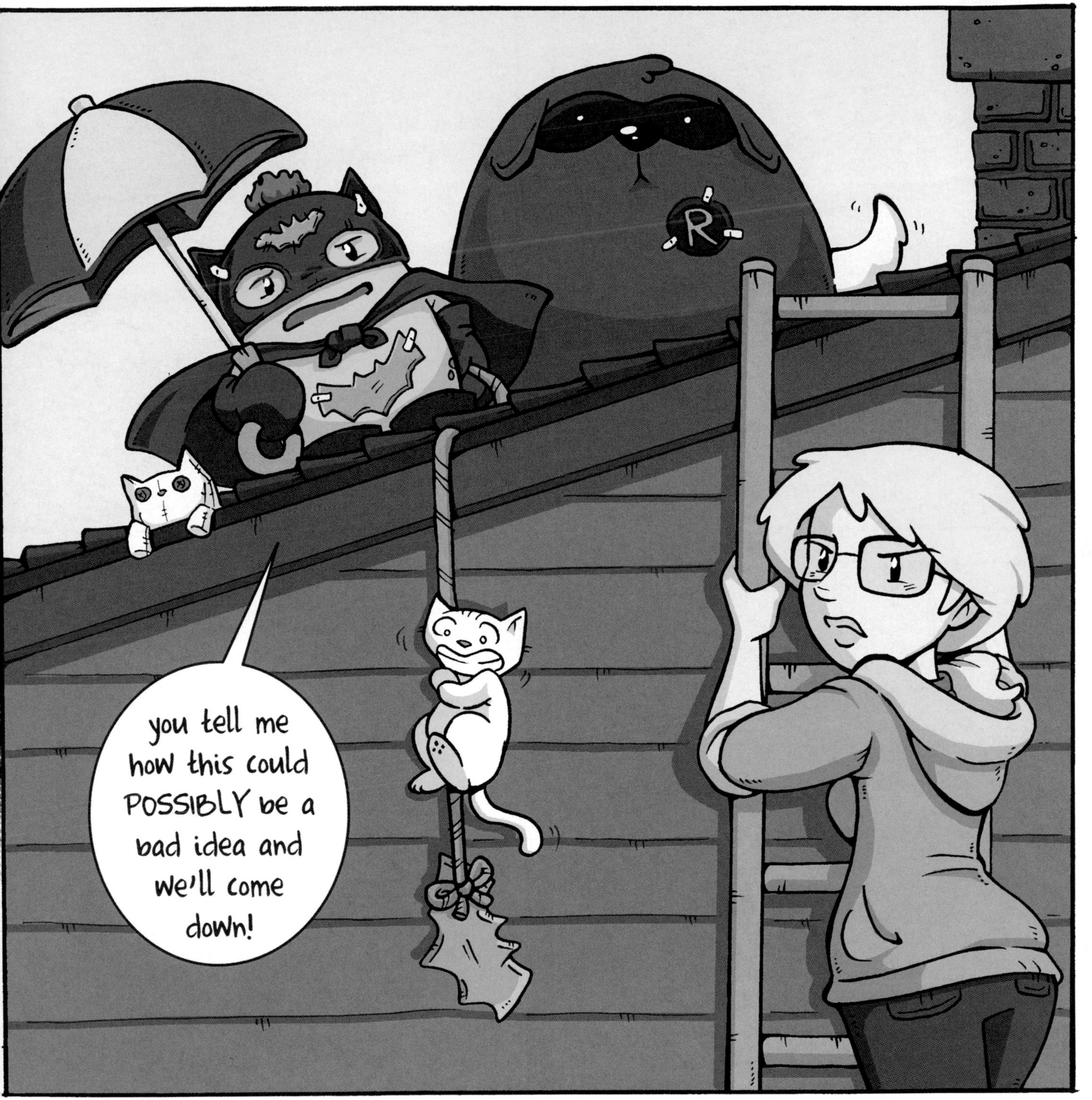
you tell me how this could POSSIBLY be a bad idea and we'll come down!

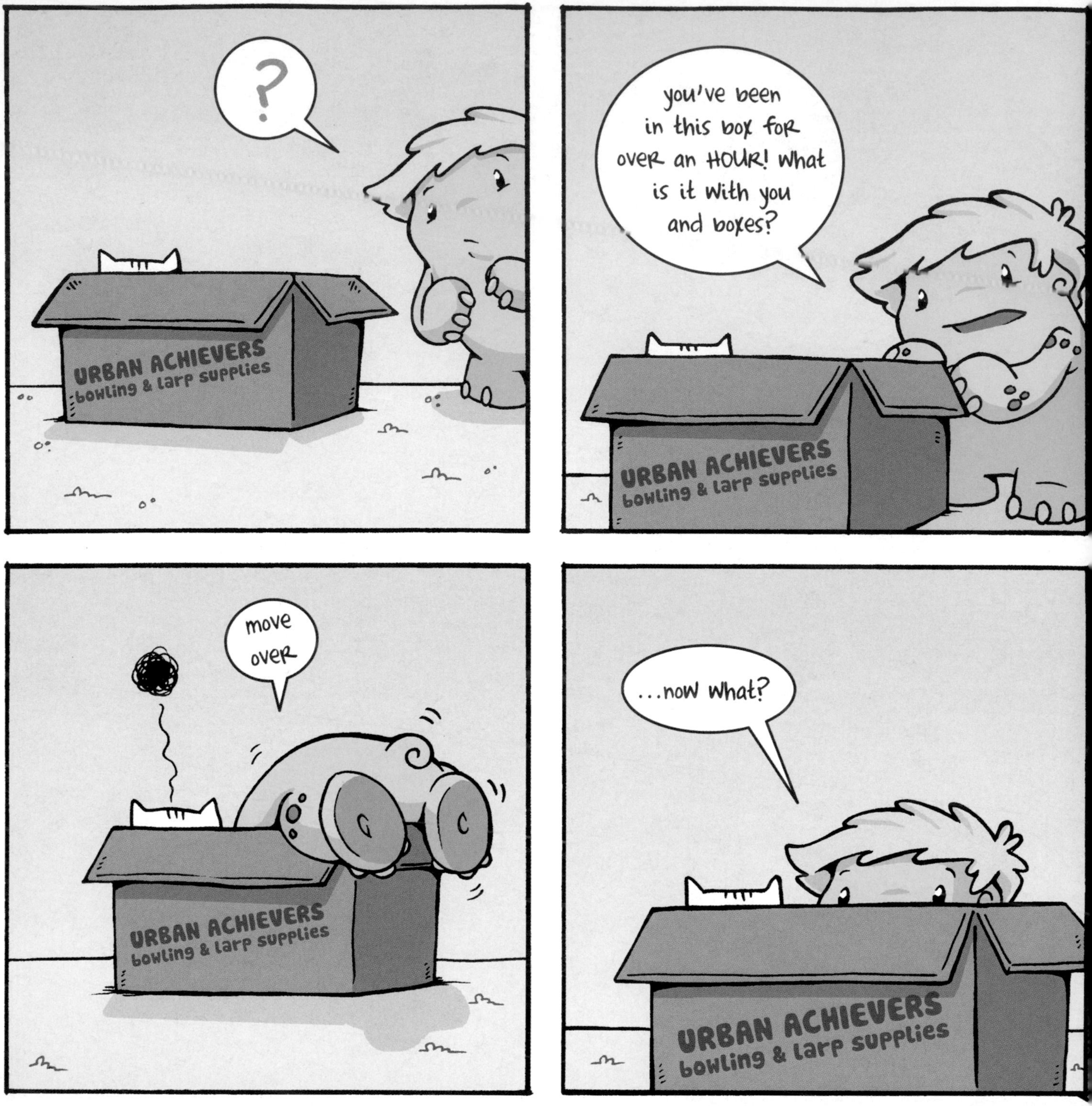
?
URBAN ACHIEVERS
bowling & larp supplies
you've been in this box for over an HOUR! What is it with you and boxes?
URBAN ACHIEVERS
bowling & larp supplies
move over
URBAN ACHIEVERS
bowling & larp supplies
...now what?
URBAN ACHIEVERS
bowling & larp supplies

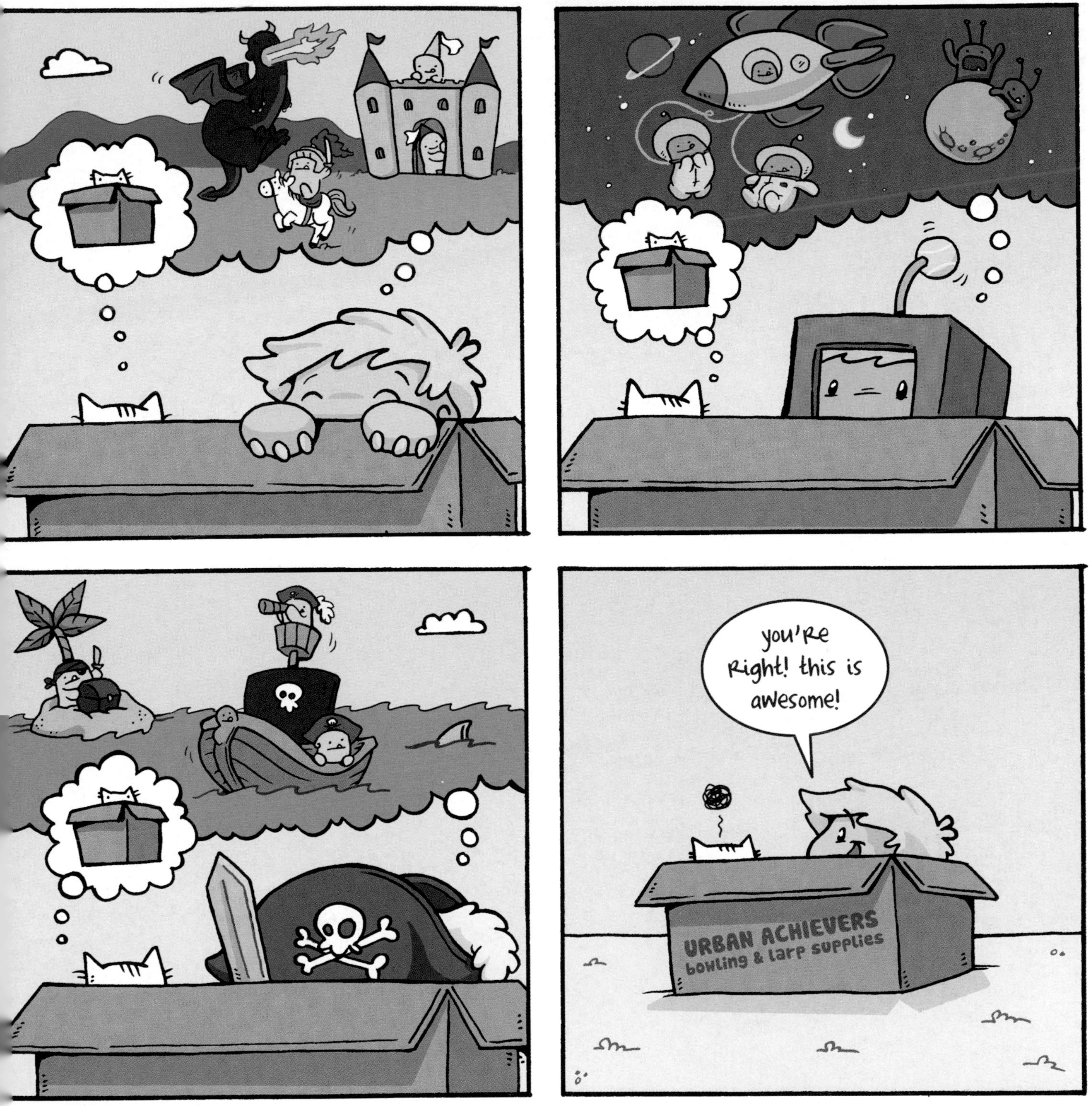
you're
Right! this is
awesome!
URBAN ACHIEVERS
bowling & larp supplies

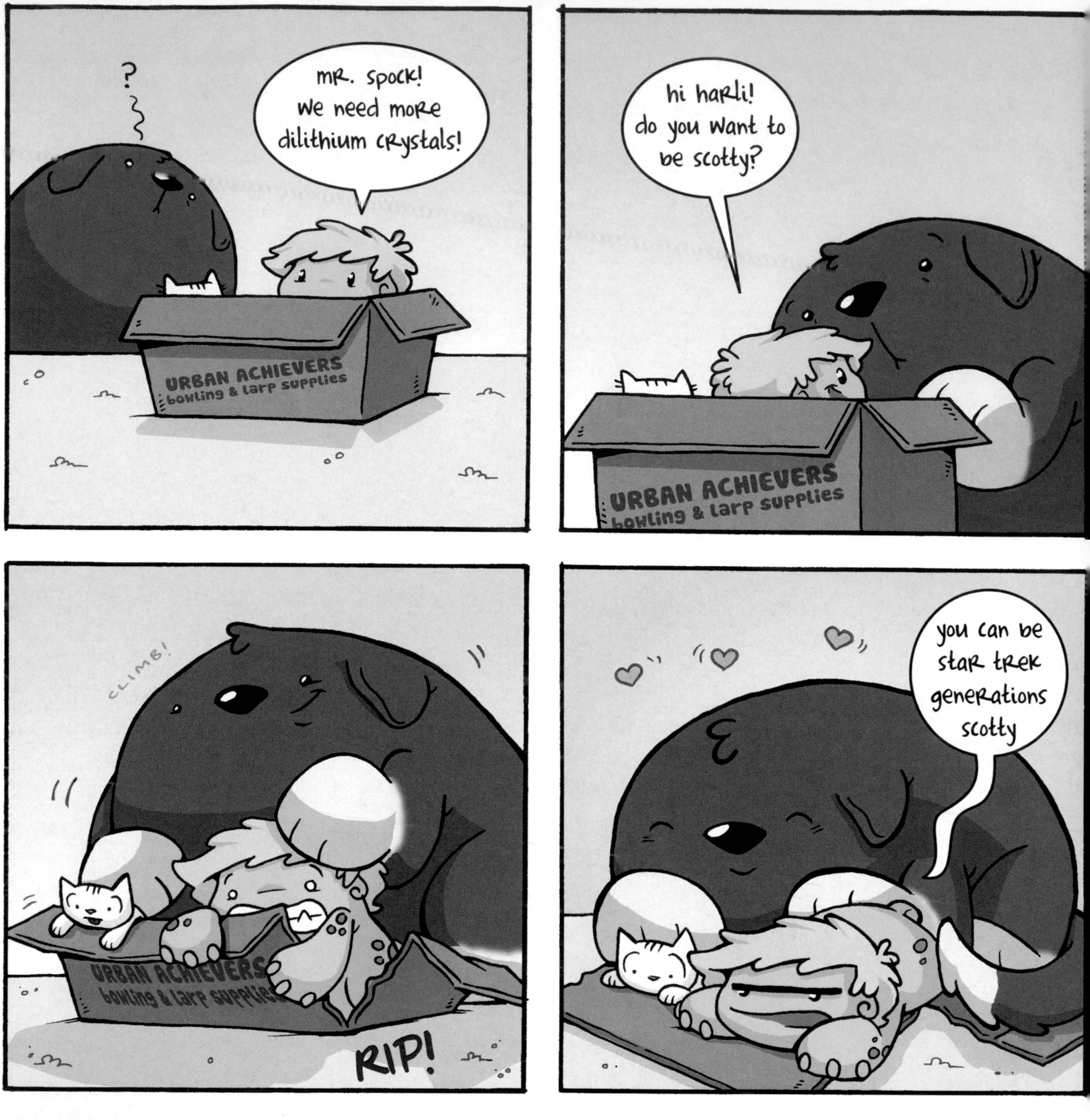
?
mr. spock! we need more dilithium crystals!
URBAN ACHIEVERS bowling & larp supplies
hi harli! do you want to be scotty?
URBAN ACHIEVERS bowling & larp supplies
CLIMB!
URBAN ACHIEVERS bowling & larp supplies
RIP!
you can be star trek generations scotty

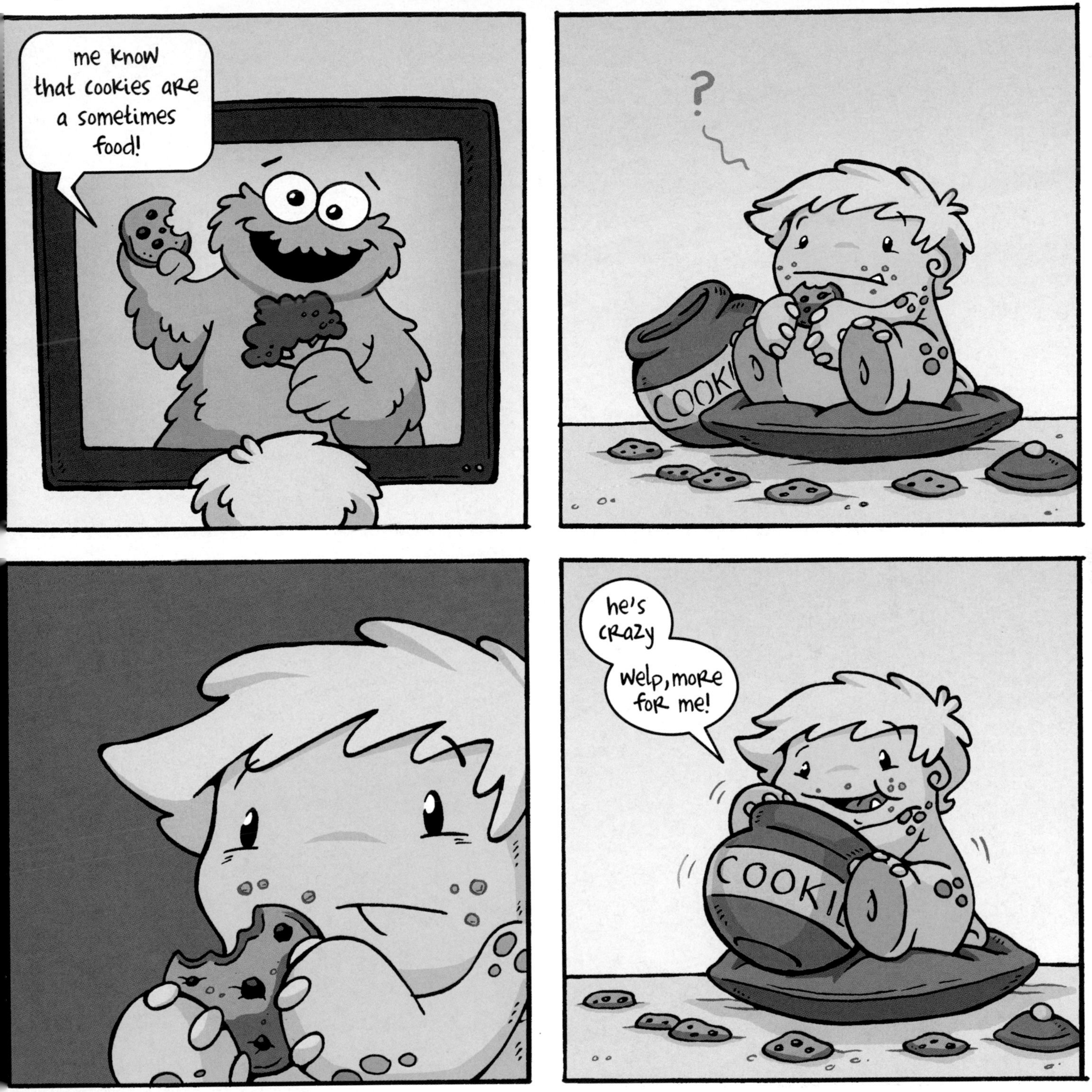
me know that cookies are a sometimes food!
?
COOKI
COOKI
he's crazy
welp, more for me!

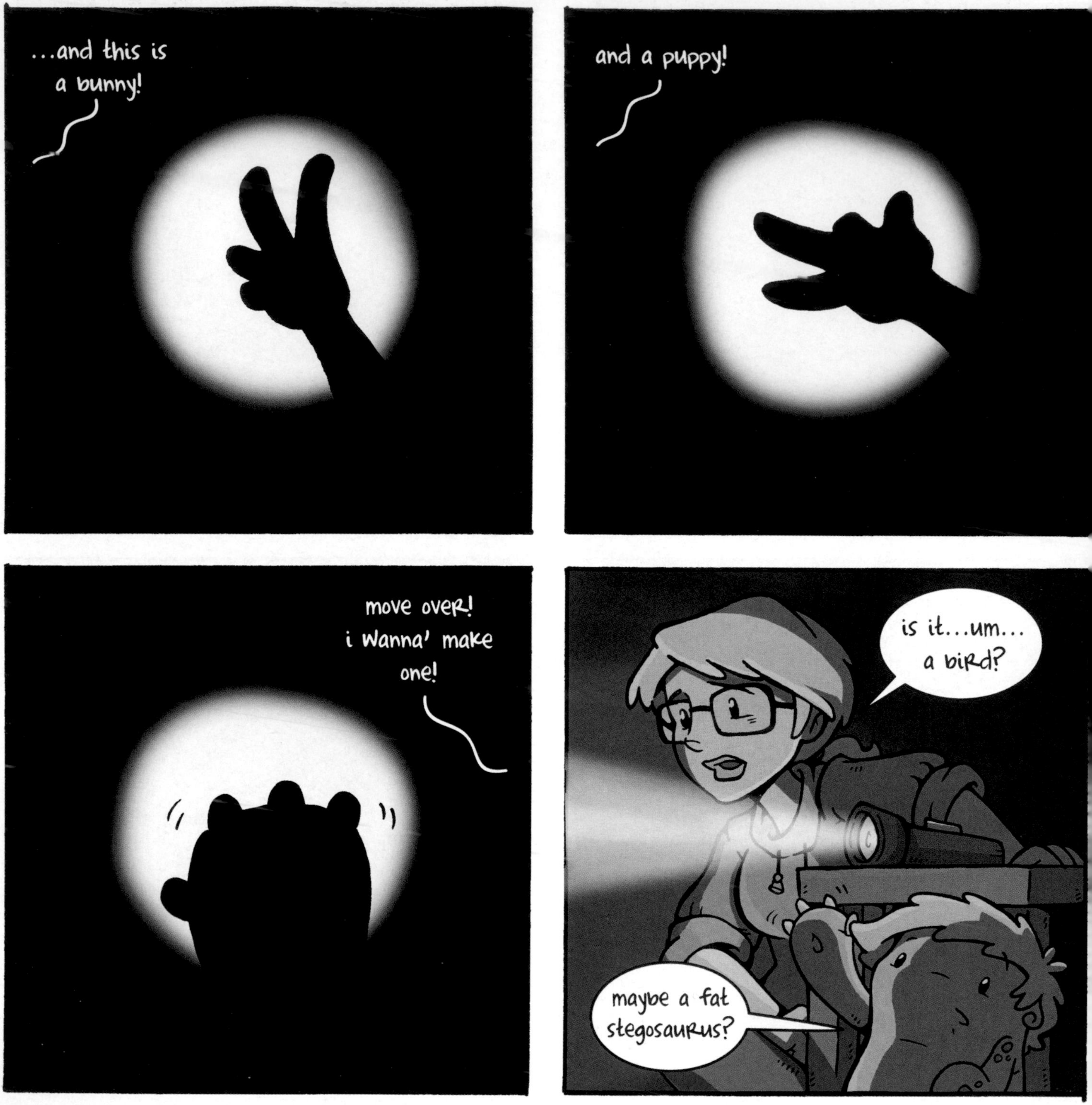
...and this is a bunny!
and a puppy!
move over! i wanna' make one!
is it...um... a bird?
maybe a fat stegosaurus?

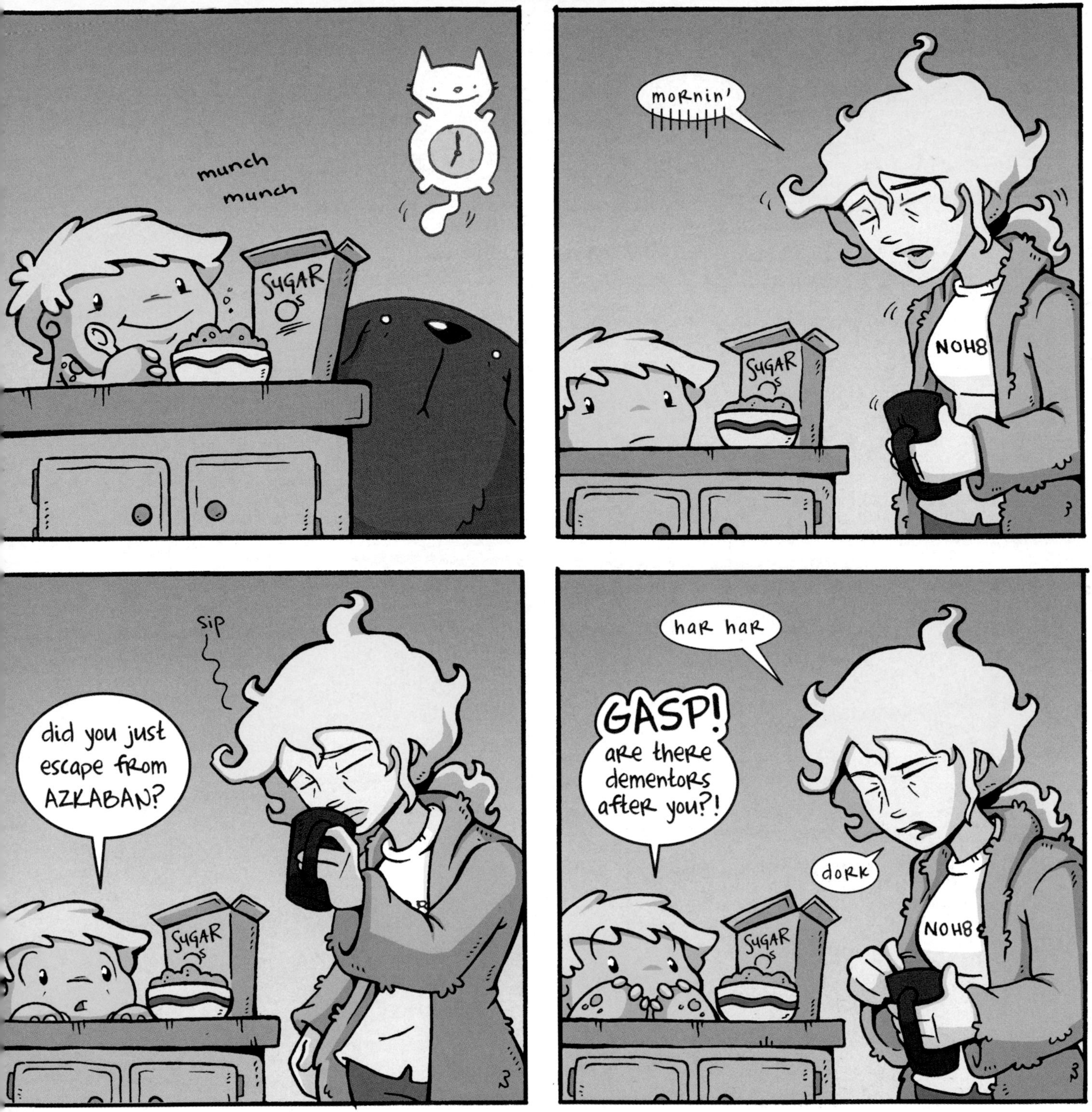
munch
munch
SUGAR O's
mornin'
NOH8
SUGAR O's
sip
did you just escape from AZKABAN?
SUGAR O's
har har
GASP! are there dementors after you?!
dork
NOH8
SUGAR O's

the story of GRONK

Gronk started out as a little monster doodle all the way back in 2000. She creeped up in my sketchbooks from time to time. Back then, she was a lot taller and leaner. Then, in 2002, I had to do a class project in college. We were to do a self-portrait, so I took that monster and rounded her out a bit, gave her my haircut and went to town drawing **PAGES** of little drawings starring her! I said for years I was going to do a book or comic starring her one day... then in 2010, I finally hunkered down and started it... it... uh...only took me the better part of a decade to get it done.

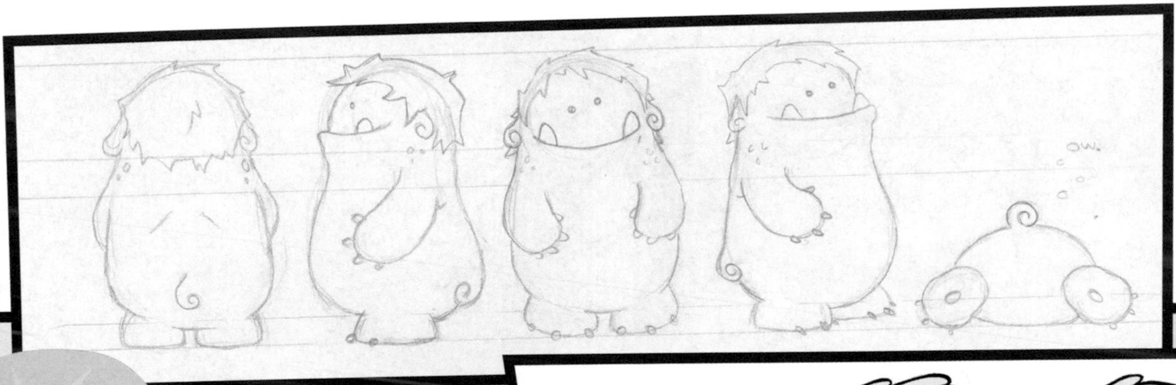
ow.

the first turnaround of gronk from 2002!

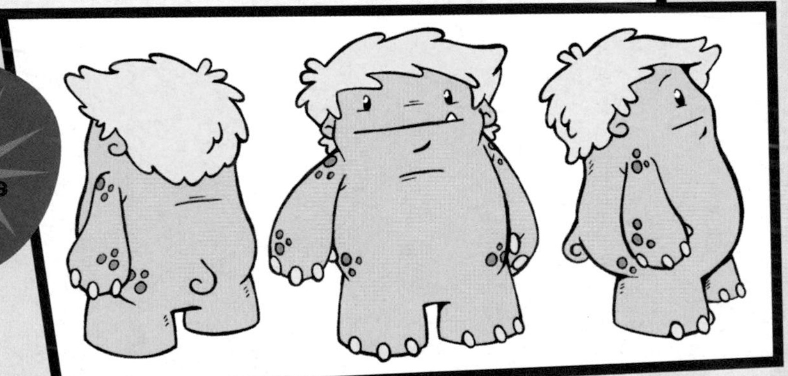

gronk as she appears now!

fun fact
gronk's name was almost "pooter"

art by jay fosgitt

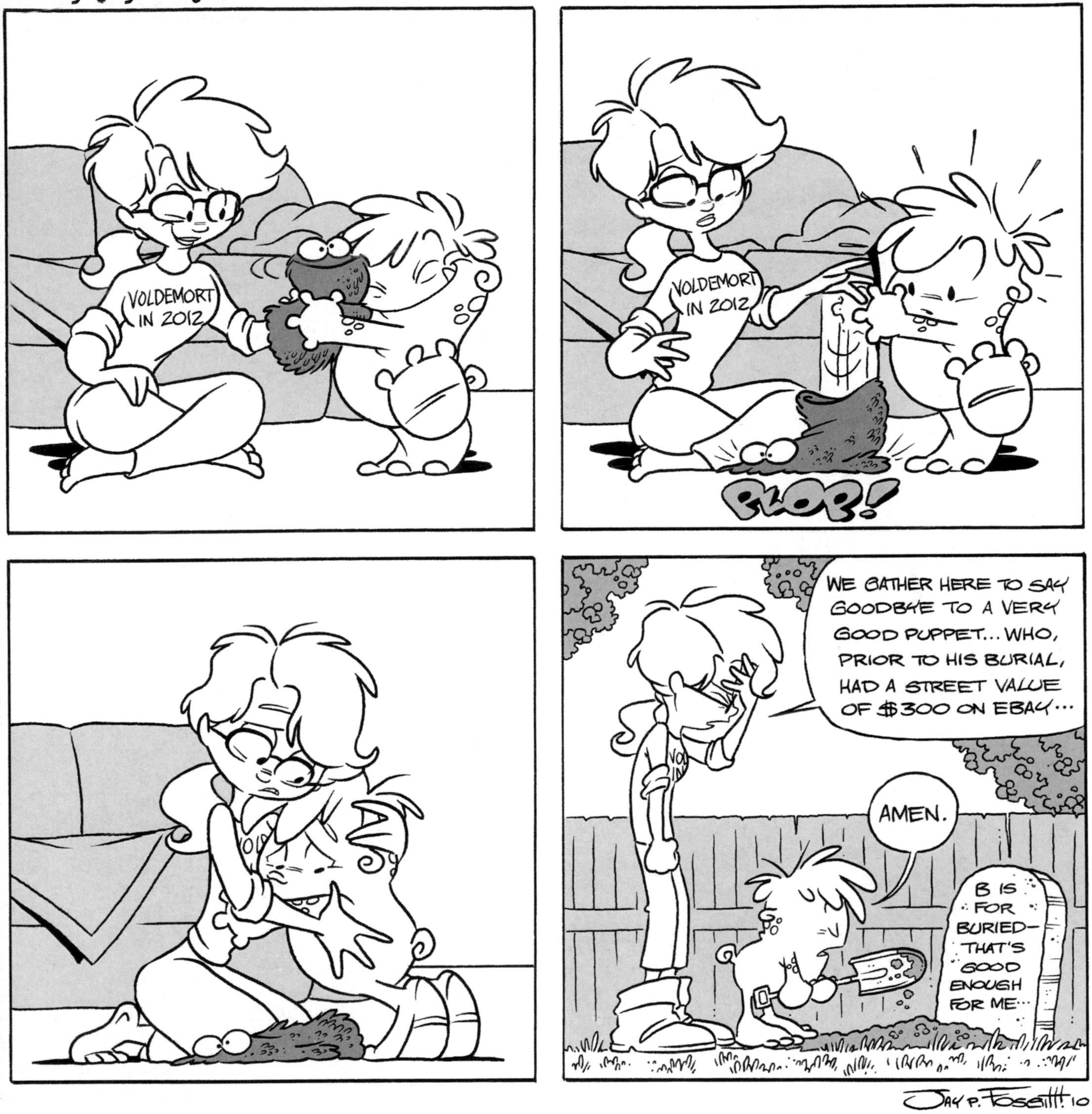
VOLDEMORT IN 2012
VOLDEMORT IN 2012
PLOP!
WE GATHER HERE TO SAY GOODBYE TO A VERY GOOD PUPPET... WHO, PRIOR TO HIS BURIAL, HAD A STREET VALUE OF $300 ON EBAY...
AMEN.
B IS FOR BURIED—THAT'S GOOD ENOUGH FOR ME...
JAY P. FOSGITT '10

art by jay fosgitt

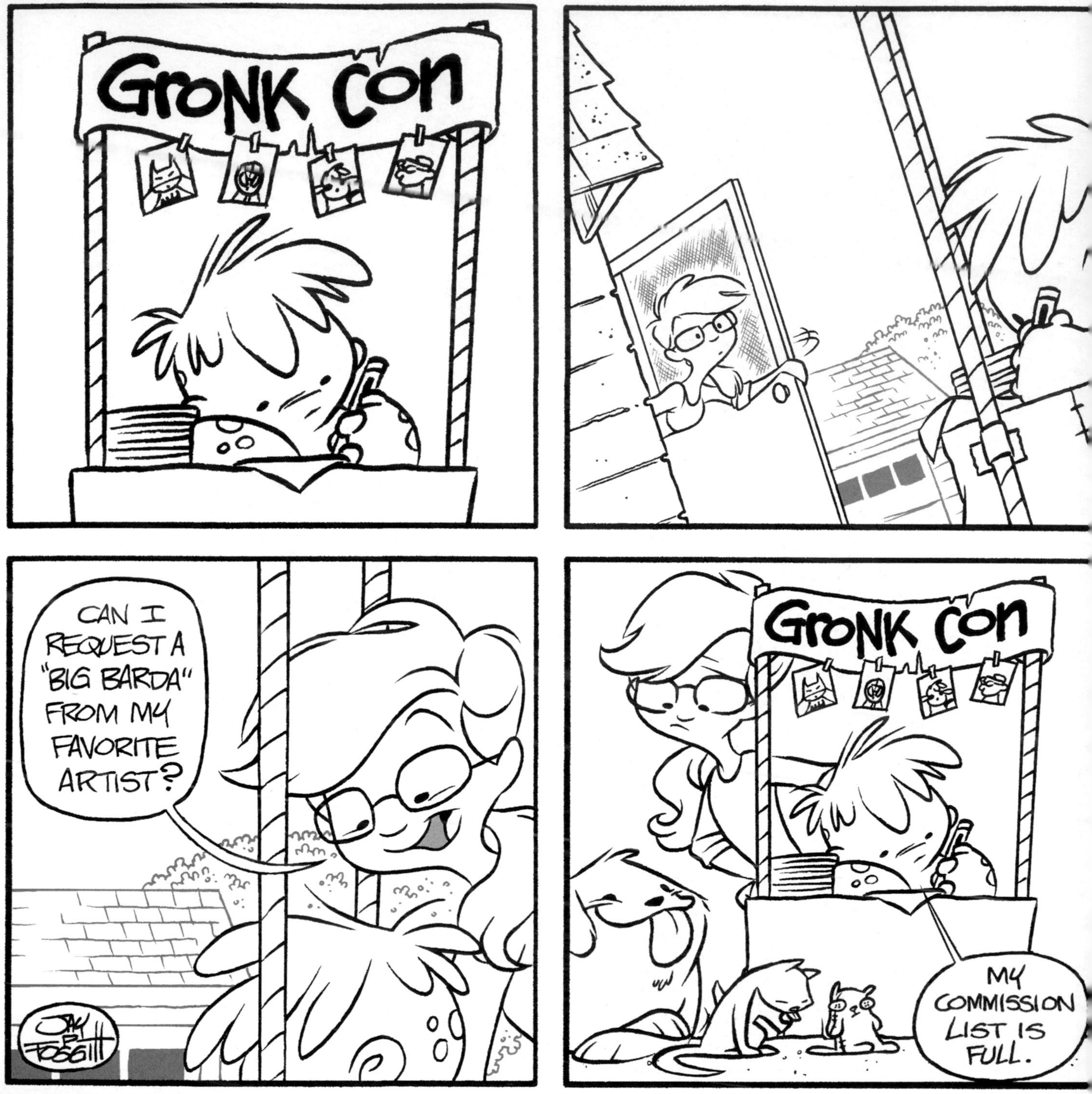
GRONK CON
CAN I REQUEST A "BIG BARDA" FROM MY FAVORITE ARTIST?
JAY FOSGITT
GRONK CON
MY COMMISSION LIST IS FULL.

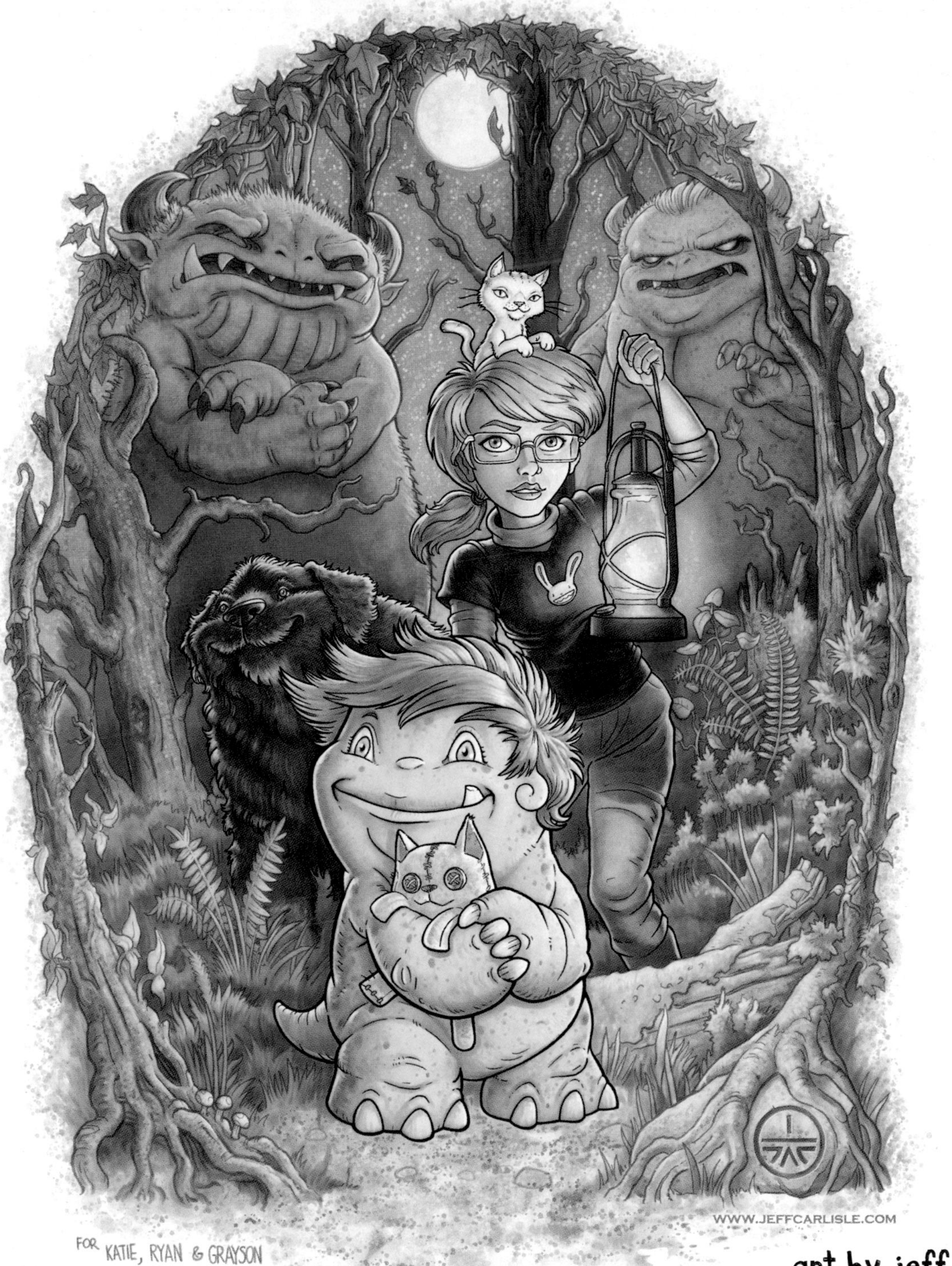
WWW.JEFFCARLISLE.COM
FOR KATIE, RYAN & GRAYSON

art by jeff carlisle

art by mike maihack

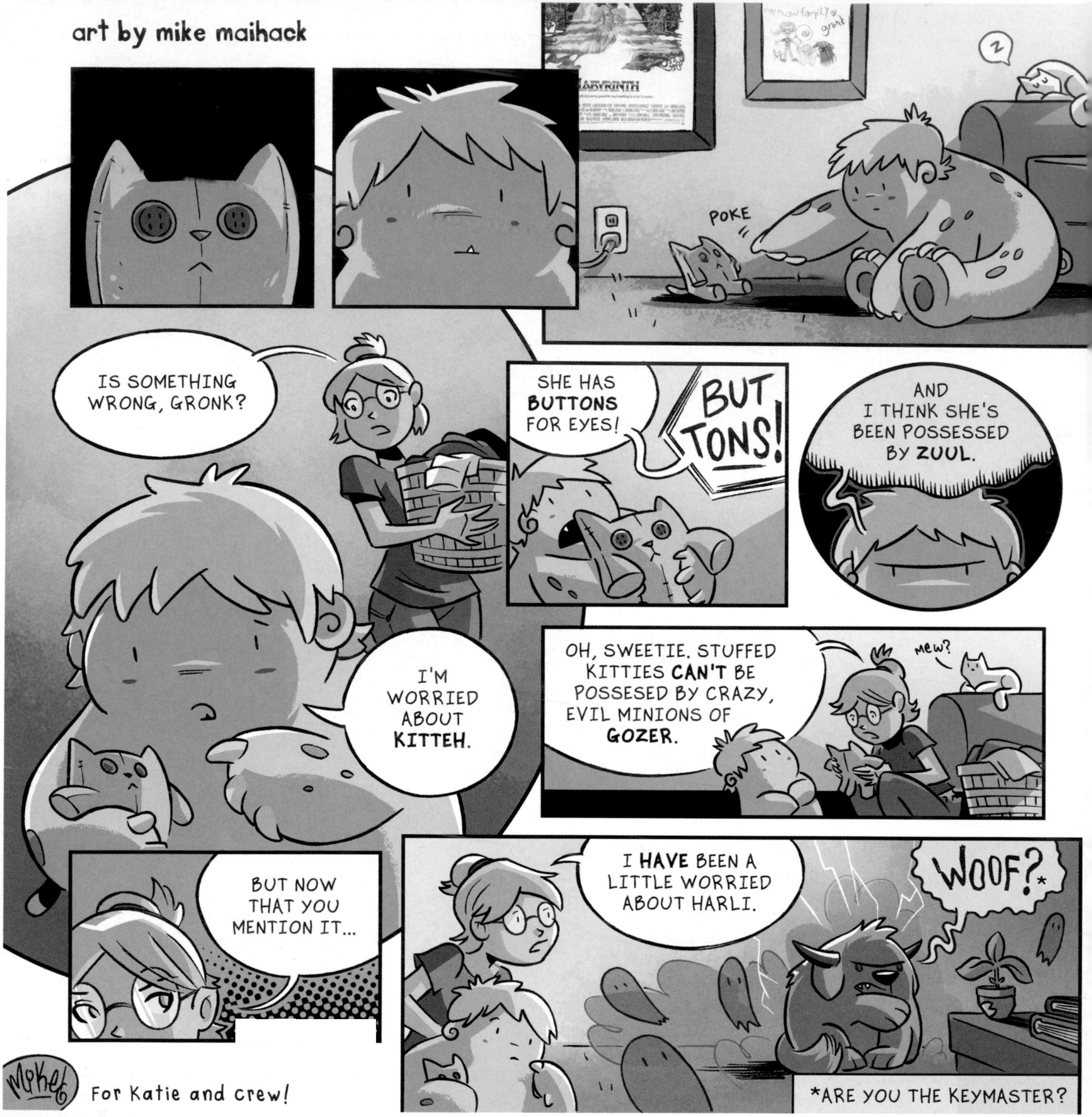

POKE
IS SOMETHING WRONG, GRONK?
SHE HAS BUTTONS FOR EYES!
BUT TONS!
AND I THINK SHE'S BEEN POSSESSED BY ZUUL.
I'M WORRIED ABOUT KITTEH.
OH, SWEETIE. STUFFED KITTIES CAN'T BE POSSESED BY CRAZY, EVIL MINIONS OF GOZER.
mew?
BUT NOW THAT YOU MENTION IT...
I HAVE BEEN A LITTLE WORRIED ABOUT HARLI.
WOOF?*
*ARE YOU THE KEYMASTER?

For Katie and crew!

art by john "super ugly" wllliams

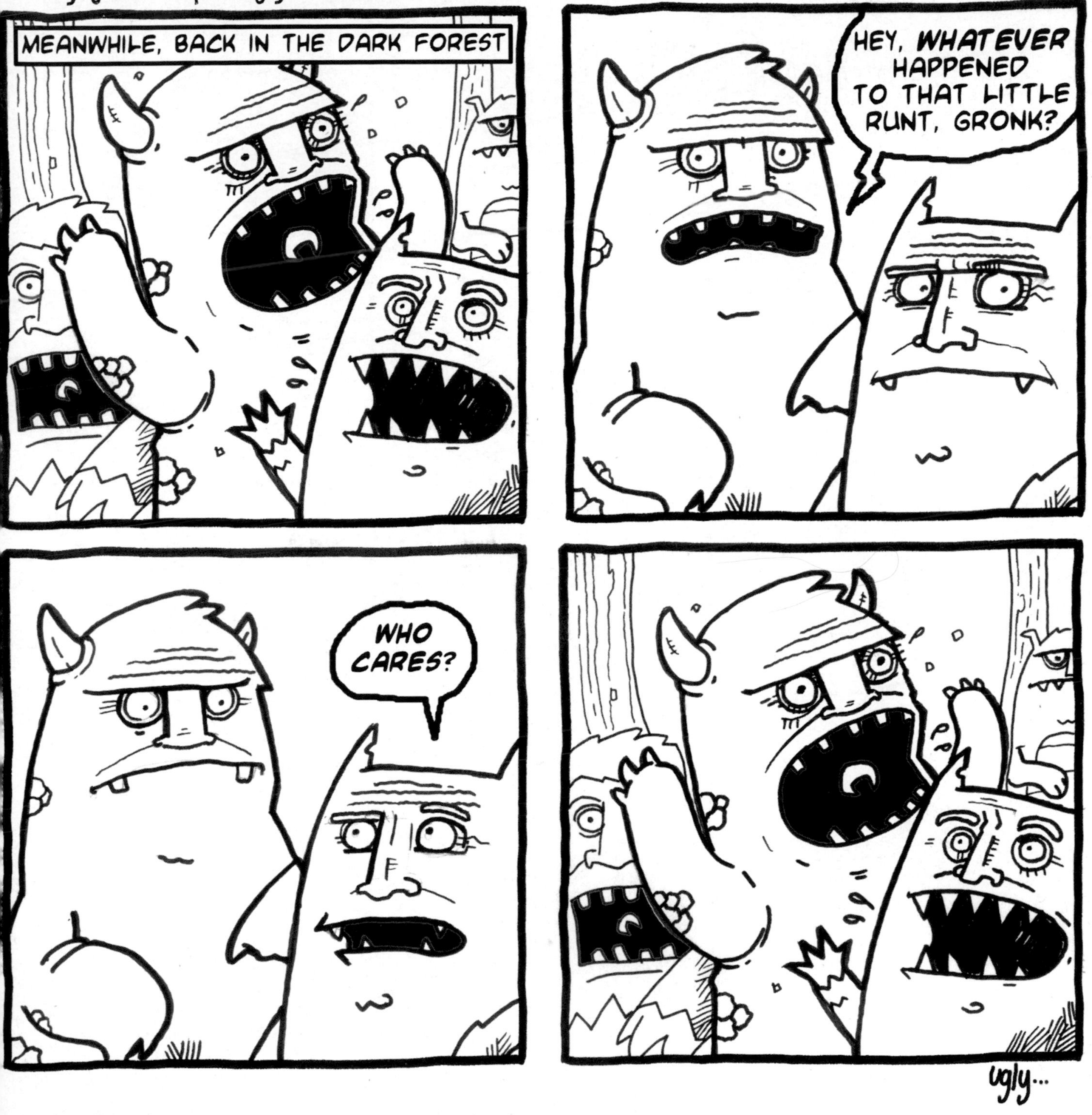

MEANWHILE, BACK IN THE DARK FOREST
HEY, WHATEVER HAPPENED TO THAT LITTLE RUNT, GRONK?
WHO CARES?
ugly...

art by jim miller

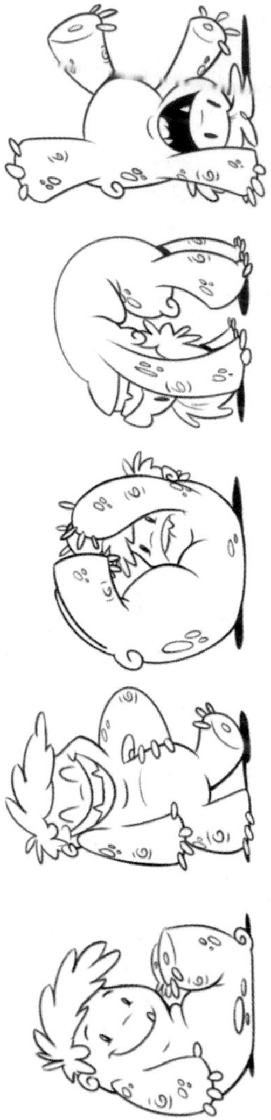

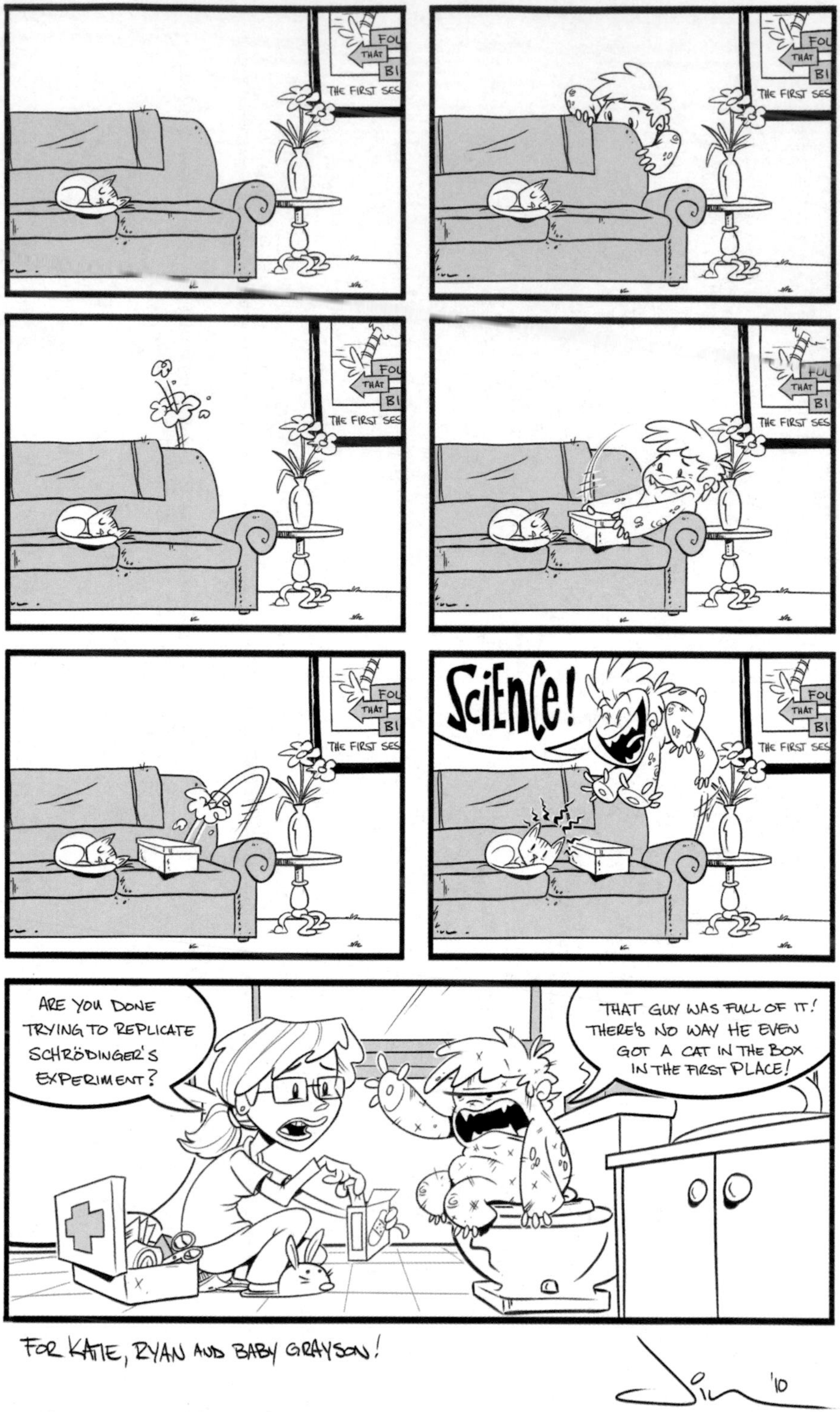
SCIENCE!
ARE YOU DONE TRYING TO REPLICATE SCHRÖDINGER'S EXPERIMENT?
THAT GUY WAS FULL OF IT! THERE'S NO WAY HE EVEN GOT A CAT IN THE BOX IN THE FIRST PLACE!
FOR KATIE, RYAN AND BABY GRAYSON!
Jim '10

GRONK

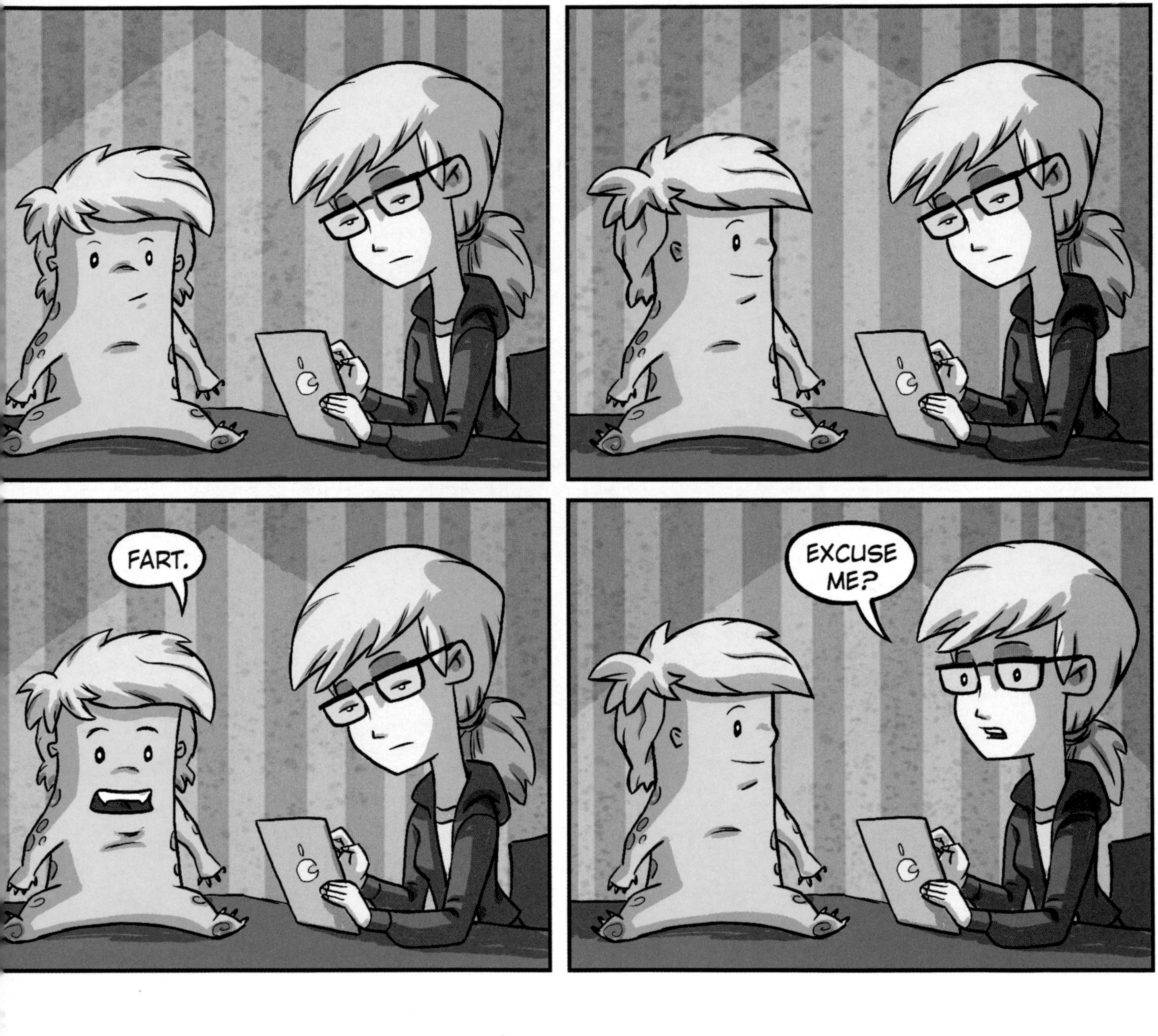
FART.
EXCUSE ME?

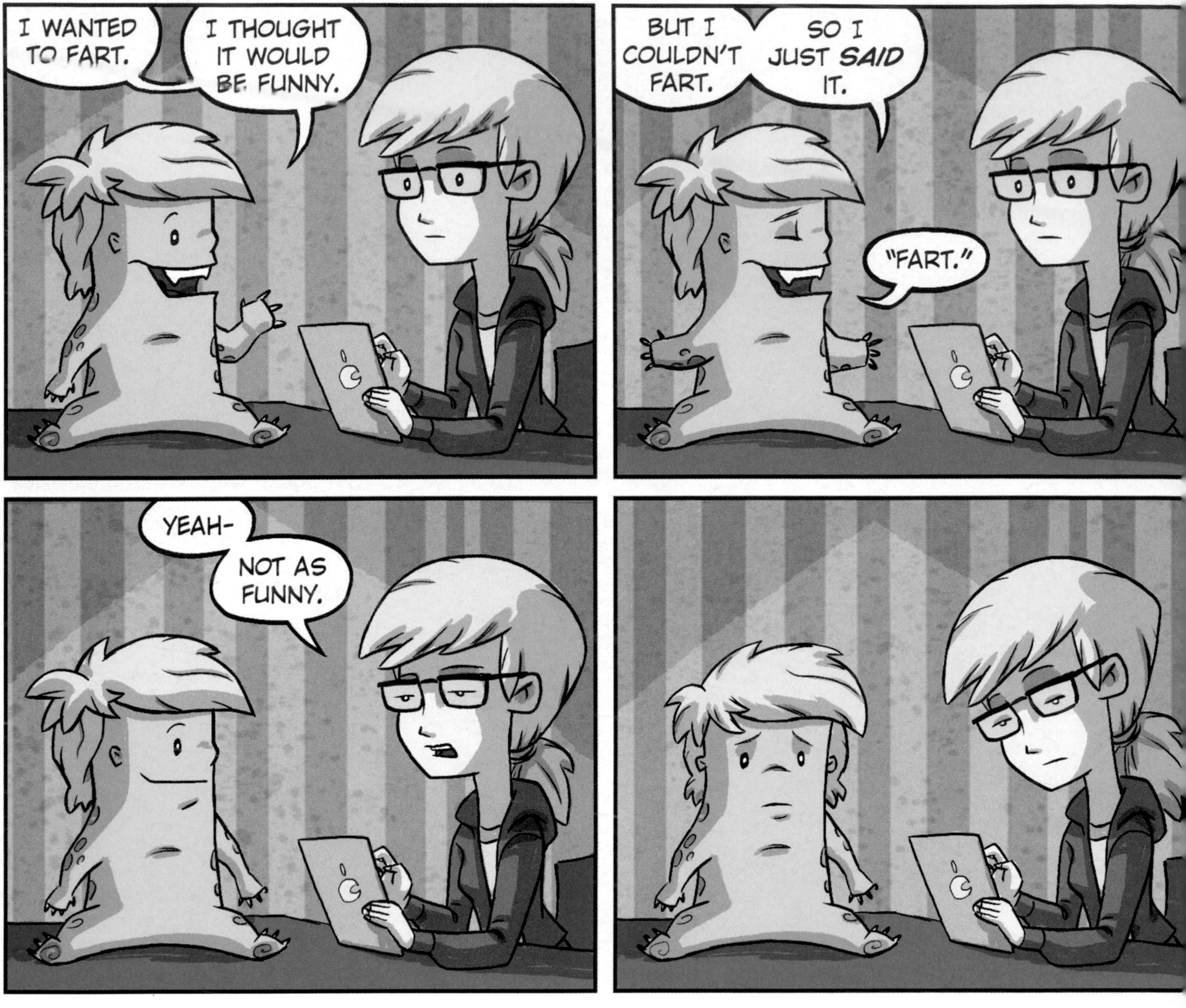
I WANTED TO FART.
I THOUGHT IT WOULD BE FUNNY.
BUT I COULDN'T FART.
SO I JUST *SAID* IT.
"FART."
YEAH-
NOT AS FUNNY.

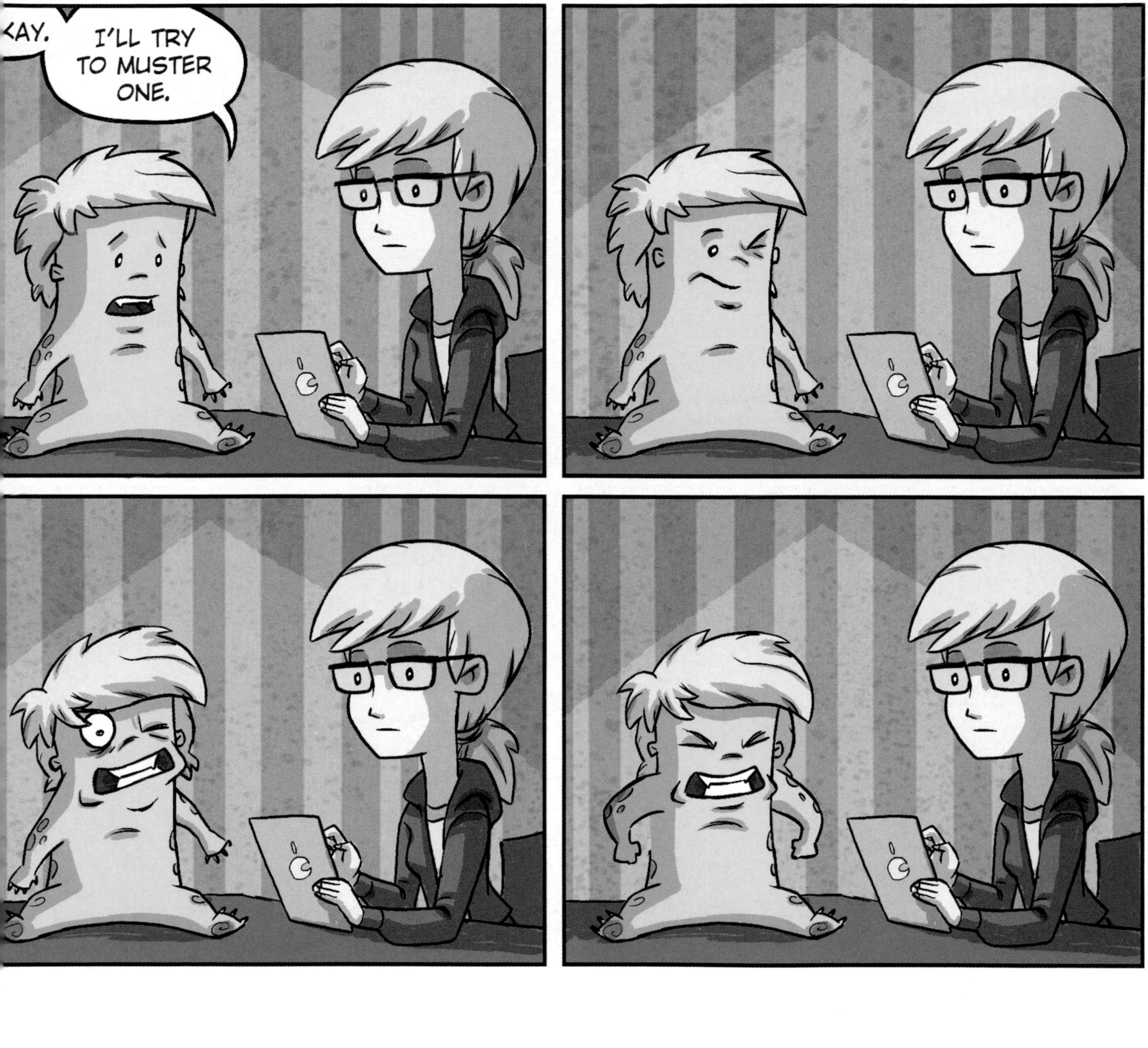
AY.
I'LL TRY TO MUSTER ONE.

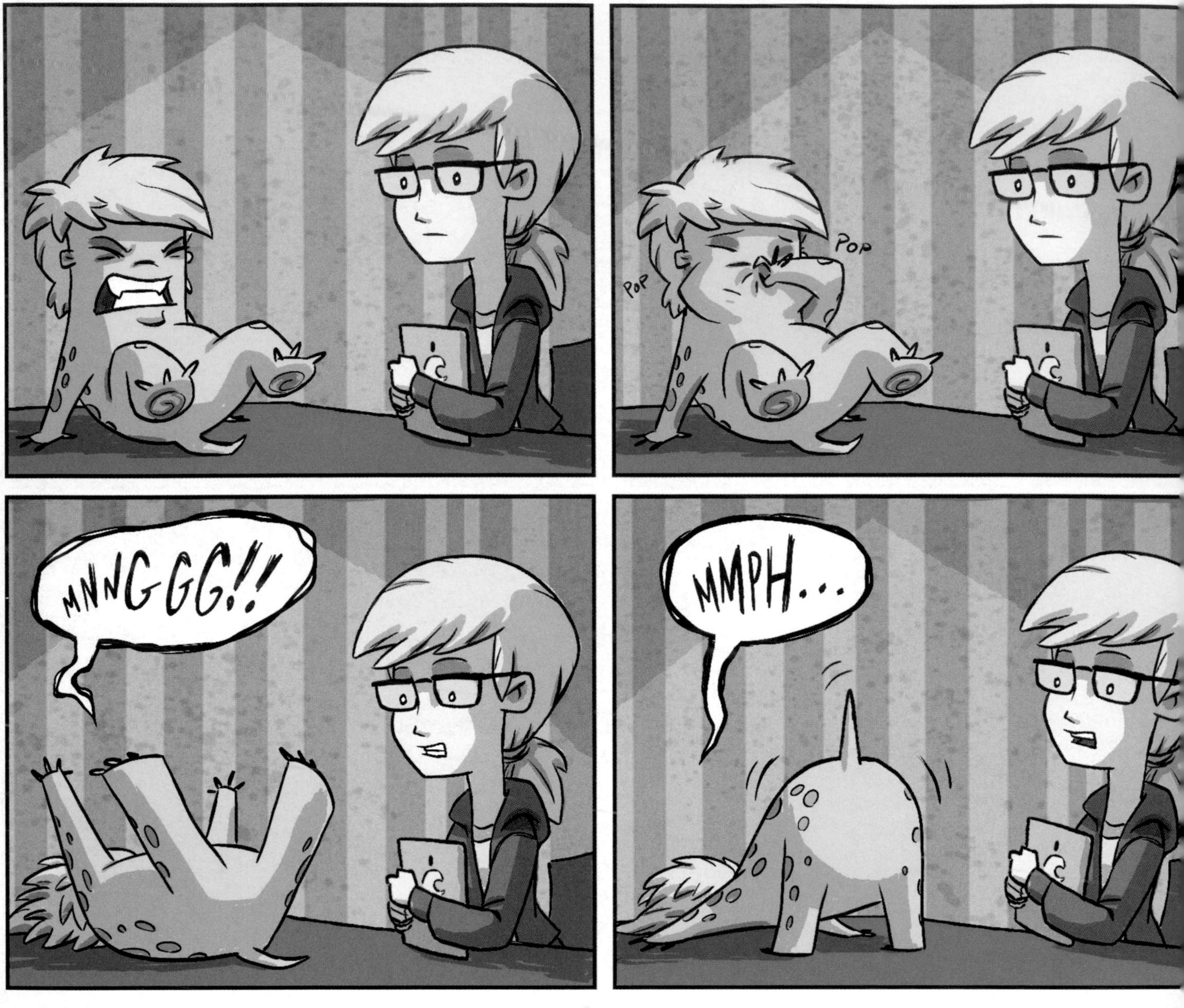
POP
POP
MNNGGG!!
MMPH...

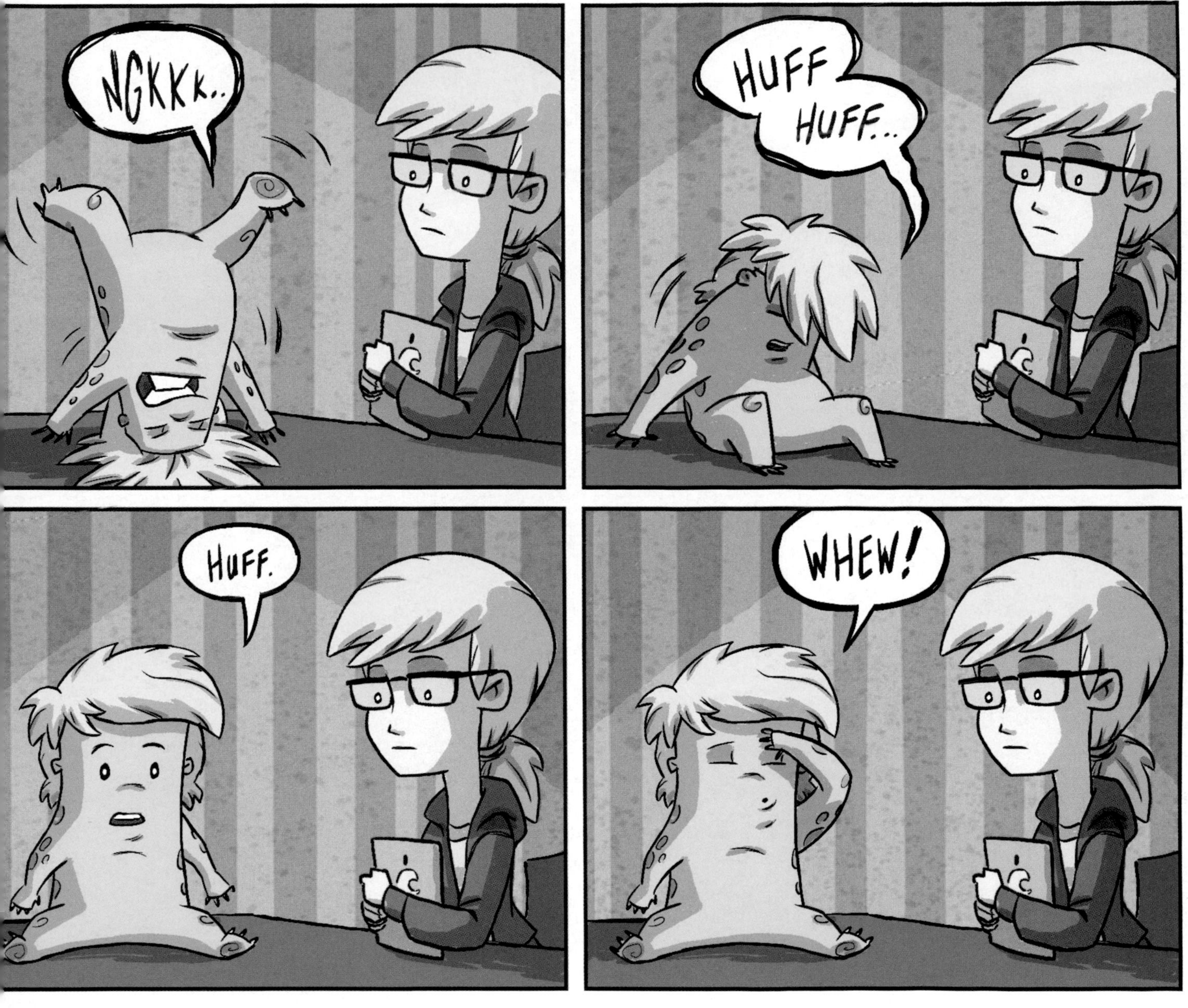
NGKKK..
HUFF HUFF...
HUFF.
WHEW!

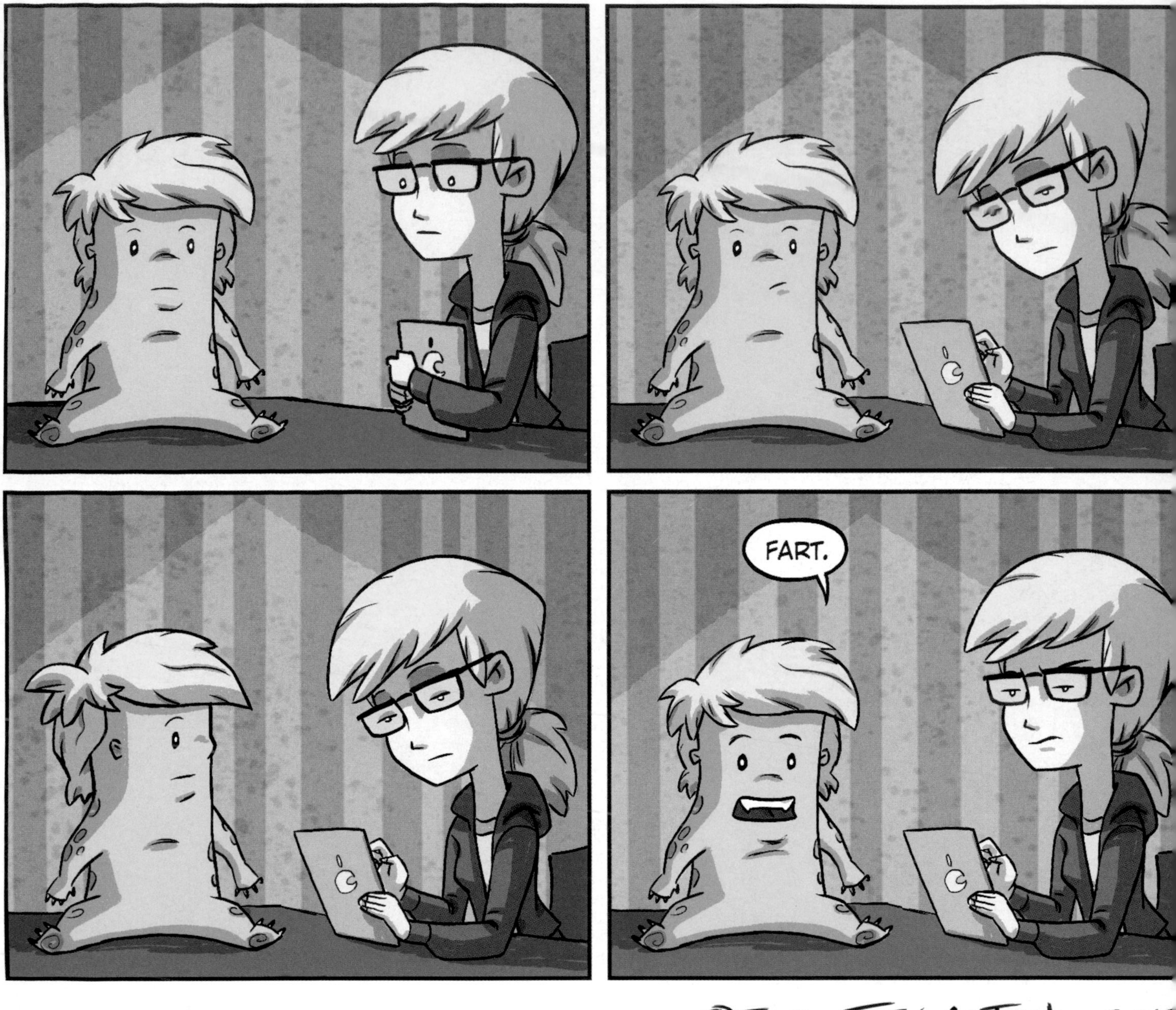
FART.

OTIS FRAMPTON 201

art by evan "doc" shaner

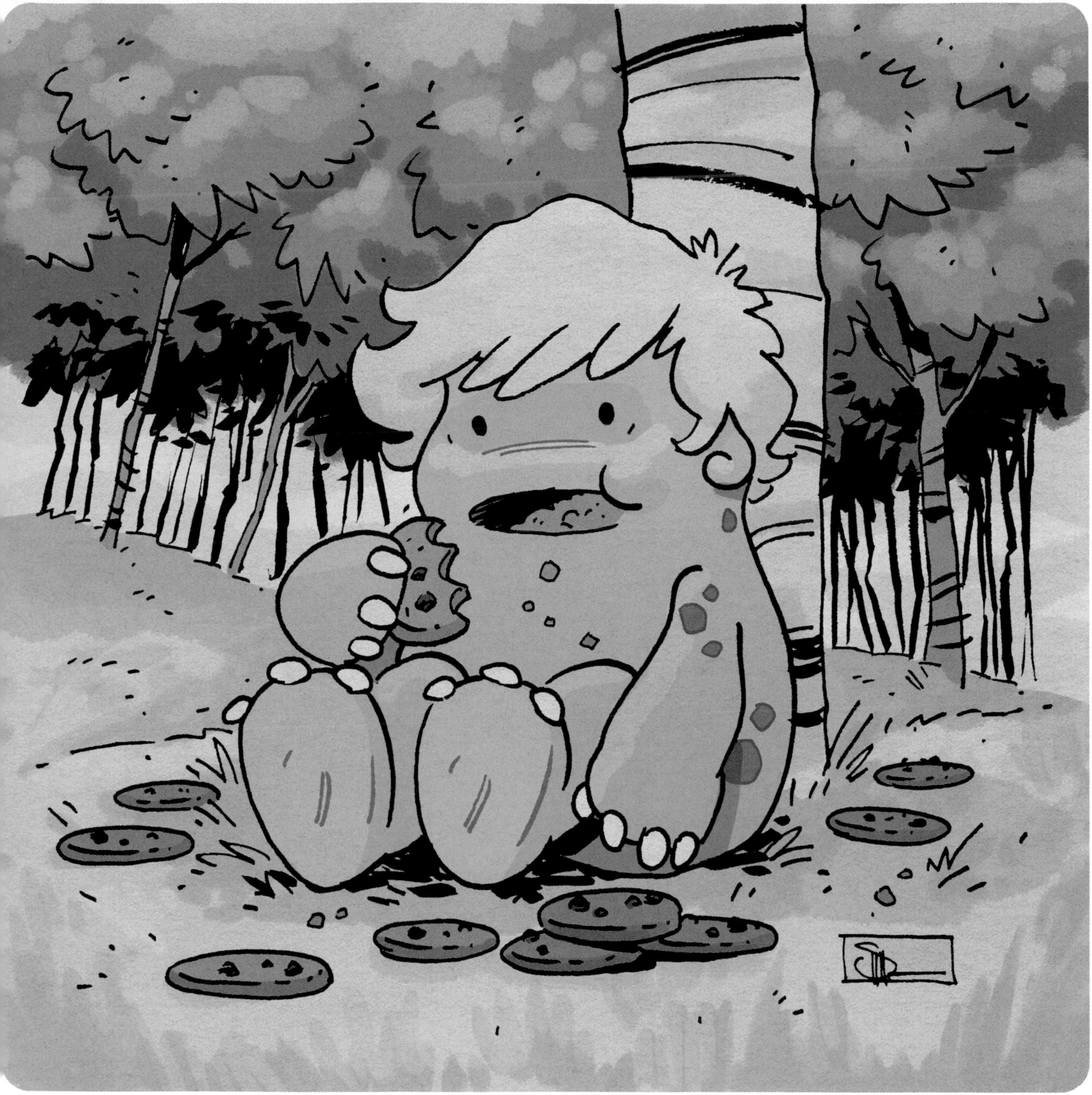

art by jamie cosley

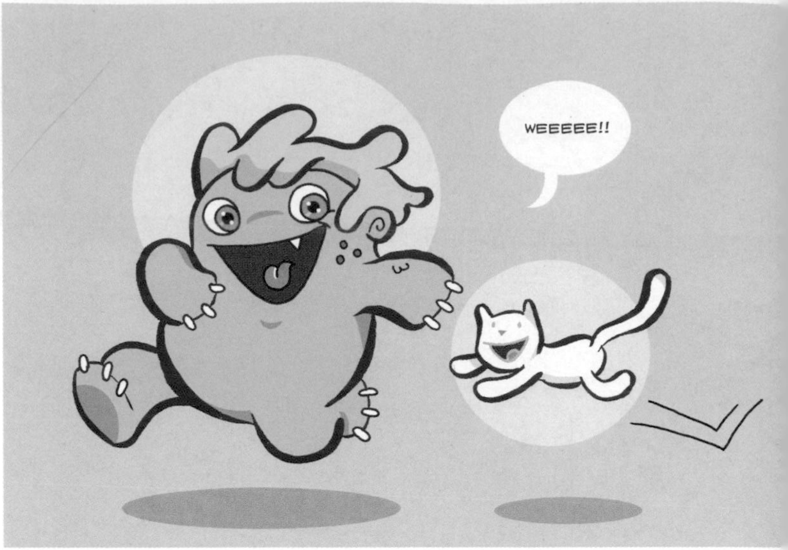
WEEEEEE!!

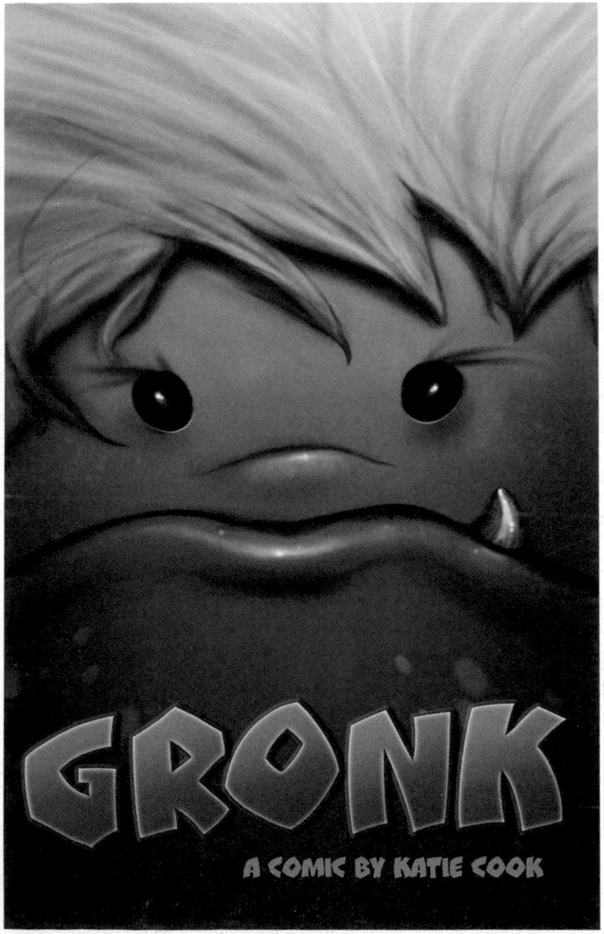
GRONK
A COMIC BY KATIE COOK

a big thank you to
ALL the folks who
have sent me such
wonderful art since
i started this comic!

-katie

art by scott harben